RETURN TO THRAE

By

Judith Galardi

This book is a work of fiction. Places, events, and situations in this story are purely fictional. Any resemblance to actual persons, living or dead, is coincidental.

ISBN: 1-4033-0815-2 (E-book)
ISBN: 1-4033-0816-0 (Paperback)

This book is printed on acid free paper.

1stBooks - rev. 06/13/03

Dedication

This book is dedicated to my daughter, Christina, my niece Lesley, my friend Evalyn, my husband Jim Sahovey, and in loving memory of my sister Diane, my mother, Marie, and my father, Richard.

Table of Contents

Part I

Judith Galardi

Finding Out

"You grew up like every other human – almost," said Laney's older brother, Phil, as they waited for the rest of the family to come into the living room for their family meeting. Then he smiled a generous smile and his brown eyes glistened. He was eighteen years old and Laney really couldn't tell if he was kidding, as usual, or not.

"What do you mean 'almost'?" Laney asked with laughter in her voice.

"Sure, you have brothers and a sister, but we really aren't your brothers and sister at all," Phil responded. He was still smiling but his voice got a little more serious.

"But I remember when David and Eileen were little," said Laney. What are you trying to tell me? That I was cloned or something?"

"Well, not exactly," replied Phil. Now there was laughter in his voice. "Don't you remember when you were in the third grade and you thought the blackboard was getting blurred, so Dad took you to get glasses?"

"Yes," Laney answered. "But what does that have to do with being cloned?"

"One thing at a time, Laney," said Phil. "You see, the blackboard wasn't getting blurred. You were disintegrating the chalk."

"Disintegrating the chalk!" Suddenly Laney was more concerned with disintegration than her possible cloning. "Are you sure?" she asked.

"Of course I'm sure," replied Phil. Laney remembered the team of scientists who were brought in. The whole class got an extra play period.

"Why do you think there were engineers in the classroom the next day? And why do you think your glasses are tinted that off-shade of gray?" he asked. "To prevent you from disintegrating anything else."

Laney touched her glasses, then quickly took her hand away.

"Do you mean that if I take off my glasses I could disintegrate something?"

"Yes," said Phil, "but don't. Mom and Dad will explain what I can't."

Their parents walked into the room. So did their younger brother, David, and younger sister, Eileen. Her parents could tell from Laney's expression that she was confused. They told her that she shouldn't be confused or afraid — they would explain everything as best they could. Laney just sat there and got more afraid.

Finally, her father said, "Phil, I don't know what you've told her, but I can't blame you for letting her know a little. You never could keep a secret until the very end. But, Laney, before I tell you, please believe me, you're our daughter. You belong with us, but, well, let's start at the beginning."

Laney leaned back on the sofa and crossed her legs. She was ready to listen.

Her father told her a story about how he and her mother found her on the riverbank and she didn't look human at all. That she was actually a mermaid of about five Earth years old. As soon as she was carried about 100 yards from the river, she changed into a human shape.

"We don't know where you're from, but we know of a place where there are people who might be able to help you find out."

Laney didn't cry when they told her that most unusual story, but they could see that she was unhappy to learn not only that she was different from the Earth children she had gotten to know, but that she wasn't even human and they didn't know where she was from.

"A mermaid," said Laney. "Oh, Dad. This can't be for real."

"It is for real," her father said. "Laney, there's nothing to be afraid of, or upset about, although it's understandable if you are. We're taking you to a special place where the staff has always known about you. We've been reporting to them since we found you. I know that seems scary to you, but don't let it be. We have even more to tell you."

Then Laney's mother spoke. "This is all so much for you to hear at once, but we thought you'd be ready by now. You're almost fourteen years old and ready to start high school."

"Then what special place are you taking me to? Why are you sending me away?"

"Oh Laney," said her father. "It's only a school – a special high school."

Laney wondered if they thought there was something wrong with her, but before she had a chance to speak her mother said: "Laney, we all love you. You're our daughter on Earth, but in the school you might learn where you're really from. The school has other high school students who are gifted, too. We'll always visit you when we're allowed. The principal told us that after you've been there a few months you will be allowed to come home and visit us on weekends. They're all ready for you. You'll have fun there. It's a very special high school where you can learn and teach."

"Me? Teach? Teach what, Mom?" asked Laney, now more interested than afraid.

"Teach them about yourself. You know now that you're not like the humans here. But you don't know how special you are. You have gifts that these doctors want to know about. They've known about you ever since we took you to buy your first pair of glasses. They wanted to take you from us then, but we wanted you to have an enjoyable childhood. They've waited all this time to work with you so that your father and I and the rest of the family could get to know you, too."

Get to know a mermaid! thought Laney. What a great bit of information all of this was to her.

"I'm confused," said Laney, "and still scared. But really surprised, too. Why did you wait so long to tell me?"

"Your father told you why," her mother said. "So you could enjoy growing up. And you did, didn't you?"

"Yes, but what about my friends? Will I ever get to see them again?" asked Laney. She was mainly concerned about her friend Michael.

"If you want to. That'll be up to you," her father said. "But you're really going to have your work cut out for you at the school. They've been waiting and receiving reports and worrying about you for the past eight years. Don't be surprised if they are eager to work with you because of it."

Laney sat quietly on the sofa, not saying anything. She just wanted to think.

"Doesn't your own silence tell you something?" Phil asked. The laughter was back in his voice and eyes again. "It tells me a lot. You're being your usual logical self. Any other thirteen-year-old would be floored, or crying, or trying to disintegrate everything in sight, but not you. You're just absorbing everything that's been said to you."

Then, Eileen jumped off her chair to the floor. She was eight years old and more mischievous than a monkey in a playpen.

Her mother gave her a stern look, but her father was ready to calm everyone down. It seemed that Eileen wasn't quite ready for this family meeting. But a family is a family, and everyone knew about Laney now.

Eileen said: "I don't believe it. She can't do anything like disintegrate things. She's different, okay? She's not from another planet. You're just saying that to scare her and me."

"Eileen is still a little too young to appreciate all of this," her father said. "There's nothing to be afraid of," he said to Eileen. "Laney is from another planet, but we don't know which one. She'll always be your big sister, won't you Laney?"

That question took Laney a while to answer. Eileen was always a bother. She sat quietly, remembering the time Eileen sneaked under her bed and tape-recorded Laney's conversation with a girlfriend. Then she made Laney pay five dollars to get the tape.

"Ahhh, Laney," her father said. "You will always be her older sister, won't you? She's a little afraid and, I think, jealous."

"I'm not jealous, Daddy. It's just weird. And I think she's weird!"

"You are jealous, aren't you, squirt?" Laney asked Eileen.

"No, I'm not!" yelled Eileen.

"Yes, you are," said Laney teasingly.

"Okay, you two," said their mother. "Laney, I expect more from you than this. Eileen just heard about all of this yesterday. We waited as long as we could to tell her because she's so young."

"I'm not too young," said Eileen. "Maybe I'm jealous, too. Go ahead, Laney, let me see you disintegrate something."

"It's okay, Laney. I have something just for this occasion," said her father. "Take your glasses off and just stare at this box."

Laney's father handed her a beautiful small box made out of marble. It had two stones glued to the top; one was red and the other was green. "But before you do, there's someone else here who needs to see you do it, too."

Meeting Dr. Bucci

An older man came into the living room.

"Laney, I'm Doctor Bucci. I'm a biophysicist. I'm one of the people you'll be working with at the school. If you don't mind, I'd like to watch."

He seemed friendly enough, but Laney wasn't sure she wanted to study with a biophysicist or anyone else who believed she could disintegrate things with her eyes.

Finally, she said, "Okay, but I don't know what you'll see."

"Oh, but I do," said Dr. Bucci. "I've been waiting a long time for this. I know what's going to happen. You're not afraid, are you?"

"Not any more," she said. "Here goes."

She took off her glasses and stared at the box. At first, nothing happened. About thirty seconds later, the red stone started to swell, pulsate and glow. Then it disappeared. The green stone did the same thing. Then, in the design of the marble she saw something she couldn't distinguish. Yes! Yes, she could. She saw a human-like figure.

It hadn't been there at first. She stopped suddenly.

"What's wrong?" asked Dr. Bucci. "Did something frighten you?"

As soon as Laney put on her glasses, the figure disappeared. "I saw a human, or something that looked human. Didn't you see it?" Laney asked.

Everyone in the room said no, including Dr. Bucci.

"Something that looked human," her father said. "Could that mean something, Dr. Bucci?" he asked.

"Not that I know of," Dr. Bucci responded. "Can you tell me any more?" he asked Laney.

"No, but I don't want to play this game anymore," she said.

"This isn't a game," said her father. "But maybe we should stop."

"Okay," said Dr. Bucci. "We can keep what's left of the box until school starts next week."

Laney looked up. Eileen was just staring at her. Then Laney looked at the box. The stones were gone.

"Where are the stones, Laney?" asked Eileen.

"I don't know," replied Laney. "I'm a little shaky."

"Of course you are," said Dr. Bucci. "We know that it takes a tremendous effort for you to do that, but you'll be all right, if our calculations are correct, in about three minutes."

"But where did the stones go?" Laney asked.

"We don't know that yet," replied Dr. Bucci. "That's why you need to come to our school, to find out. Our theory is that you convert material into energy."

"What?" Laney exclaimed, feeling less tired.

Dr. Bucci, her parents and Phil all smiled.

"That's what we thought you'd say," said Dr. Bucci. "We think you absorb the energy from these things, but we aren't sure what you do with it. You may be changing it into something else. That's what you'll be teaching us about. As you learn, we'll learn. And anything we find out, we'll explain to you."

Laney smiled. She never thought she could teach a teacher. That school sounded much better to her now.

"The stones are really gone," said Eileen. "I believe it now. Hey, Laney. Would you come to school and disintegrate my math teacher?"

After everyone stopped laughing, Dr. Bucci said, "She doesn't disintegrate people, at least we don't think she does. Have you ever looked at someone without your glasses?"

"No," said Laney, wondering jokingly if she should try to disintegrate Eileen.

"Good," said Dr. Bucci. "You'll try that at school, too. You see, we knew enough about your eyes to know that you had to have specially treated glasses to prevent you from disintegrating everything you looked at. You won't be wearing your glasses much at school during our classes with you. A lot of what you'll be doing is similar to what you just did. We have a psychologist who will try to help you remember when you first arrived and why you're here. Also, there's a medical doctor who will explain, with me, what happens when you disintegrate something."

Phil wasn't as amazed as Eileen. He just sat there looking at Laney with a very warm smile on his face.

Finally, David, the quiet ten-year-old said: "I've known about you for two years. I'm glad that you know what's been going on. You look tired. Are you sure you're okay?"

He looked a little worried, so Laney suggested that they all go out to the patio so she could get some fresh air.

"Are you upset in some way?" Dr. Bucci asked.

"No," Laney said. "But I'm still a little confused. Will I be living at the school?"

"Yes," said Dr. Bucci. "But it really will be just like high school, except that you'll be in a school where there are people of Earth who can do things that are a little out of the ordinary. Did we break all this news to you too fast?"

Laney liked Dr. Bucci even more now. He really seemed to care about her.

"Well," Laney said, as she sat down on a lawn chair, "I just feel a little stupid because I couldn't figure it out myself."

"That's my sister!" laughed Phil.

"You should know that we have a student at school named Tom who may be more intriguing than you," said Dr. Bucci, smiling.

More intriguing than me? thought Laney She was actually a little jealous, and far more interested. Now she was even more eager to try her new school. She was truly enjoying all the attention.

"Try disintegrating something else," David said. "Maybe you won't feel as bad. Maybe if you see what you can really do, you'll understand why we waited this long to tell you."

Her dad put a brick on the grass. "Do you think this will be all right, Dr. Bucci?" he asked.

"Well…." Dr. Bucci hesitated. "I was hoping to save this kind of thing for the school where the other instructors and I would have the right equipment, but – oh, go ahead. I'm just concerned about how Laney reacted when she disintegrated those stones."

"I'll be okay," she said. "If it gets too hard, I'll stop."

She took her glasses off and stared at the brick. Soon it began to glow a bright red with yellow around the edges. Then it fell into smaller pieces. Each piece was pulsating with a green light.

In the light she saw the figure again. This time Laney kept staring, but as soon as the glowing stopped the brick was gone. She put her glasses back on and closed her eyes.

"Are you all right?" she heard her mother say.

"Yes, but I saw that figure again," Laney said, keeping her eyes closed. "You have no idea where it's from?" she asked Dr. Bucci.

"No," he said with a smile, "but we'll find out soon enough. I only wish we could start you in school right now."

There was nothing on the spot where the brick disappeared. Laney was less amazed but more inquisitive.

"I know what you're going to ask, Laney," her father said. "School starts in one week. This week we just want you to relax and invite your friends over to let them know what you'll be doing."

Dr. Bucci thanked Laney and her family and said: "You'll have fun at our school, too. There will be several students there with whom you'll probably become quick friends. By the way, may I take the box to the laboratory? We can study it today."

"Be my guest," Laney's father said. "We could have lots of semi-disintegrated objects now that Laney knows. But, of course, we'll not have her do any more until she's in school."

Laney pushed her long auburn hair away from her eyes and put on her glasses.

"But you have no idea how I do it?" she asked Dr. Bucci.

"Right now, we think that you are absorbing the objects by converting them into energy," replied Dr. Bucci. "Then, we believe that you take the energy and put it into something else. But it's only a theory. We'll get to the bottom of it soon enough."

"How long will I be in the school?" Laney asked.

"At least a year," replied her mother. "But we think you'll enjoy it so much that you may want to stay even longer."

Dr. Bucci stood up, thanked everyone and walked to the door. He was happy that everything went well and told Laney's father not to worry about his wondrous daughter. Laney's father assured him again that she wouldn't disintegrate anything else! They shook hands and Dr. Bucci left.

"What do you think now, Laney?" Phil asked.

"I think I'm ready to go now," she said. "There's so much for all of us to learn."

What Laney didn't admit was that she was overwhelmed by their ability to keep her a secret and that they'd been in touch with that school for as long as she had been on Earth.

"It's all very exciting," Laney said. "But what will happen when I discover where I'm from? What must that planet be like? Is it as beautiful as this Earth? And what about my parents on that planet? Why did they send me away? Was there something wrong? Which parents will mean more to me if I ever do meet the others? And what about going back there? By way of a rocket? Does the United States have a rocket that can take me to where I'm from? Will I be able to come back here for a visit if I do go back to my other planet?"

"I wish we could answer your questions - you need to know the truth," her father replied calmly. "Hopefully, you and the staff will find it. It's scary, I know, but the truth is liberating, you'll see. Don't worry. I'm sure you'll be a real whiz kid."

The whole family prepared for dinner. Laney thought of disintegrating her food instead of eating it. Then she remembered her father's promise to Dr. Bucci. She laughed to herself and cut the lettuce for the salad. What a remarkable day this had been.

With Michael

The only friend Laney really wanted to see was Michael. They studied and went to dances and football games together. And swimming! They swam every weekend. She invited him over on Thursday, three days before she was to leave for school. After Laney told him what she had learned and what she was about to do, he just sat there with a big smile on his face.

"I already knew," he said to her. "Your parents told me about it one night before I took you swimming." Then he laughed and said: "They actually believed that you might turn into a mermaid! That's why we never raced. It seemed that the faster you swam, the easier it got for you. You just glided through the water, and your hair actually looked like it got lighter and longer. Maybe under certain circumstances you could turn into a mermaid."

"So that's why you would want to get out of the water after a short swim," Laney said.

"That's right," said Michael. "I couldn't let you swim too long or too fast. It looked like you would turn into a mermaid any minute."

Laney was surprised but not confused anymore. The family knew and so did Michael. She was glad. She was afraid he'd think she was strange – too strange to spend time with or be friends with.

"Will you come to visit me at school?" Laney asked.

"Are you kidding?" said Michael. "Sometimes, when they let you use the pool, they want me with you. They want to see the school swimming champion get beaten by a mermaid."

Laney was happier than ever. It seemed to her that Michael was actually proud to be her friend, even though she was different.

"Why didn't you ever tell me about myself?" she asked.

"Your parents wanted to be the ones," said Michael. "Hey, Lane, why do you think you never turned into a mermaid?"

"I don't know," she answered. "But they'll let me swim with you? It sounds like they really do want me to have fun while they study me. I was afraid they would treat me like some kind of guinea pig."

Michael laughed and said, "I'm surprised you're not as scared as I thought you would be. And, yes, they know what your independence means to you. They're going to let you be as free as possible while you learn."

"Will I only swim with you or can we still go out?" she asked.

"You mean you still want to go out with me?" asked Michael. "What if they bring in some dashing young genius who falls madly in love with you and you with him? Then what about me?"

"Oh Michael," said Laney. "That'll never happen. I like you a lot. You don't have to worry about that. I just don't want to give up my time with you. They won't always be around us, will they?"

Michael was surprised to hear Laney sound insecure. He liked her. One of the reasons was because of her independence.

Michael smiled again and said: "No. They said we could be alone. But guess what they asked me? They asked me what it felt like to kiss you."

"What!" she said angrily. "That's none of their business!"

"Don't be upset, Laney. It'll be that way. When they asked me, I got angry and a little embarrassed. After I refused to answer, they said they really needed to know everything about you, even that. So after they talked to me for a while I told them."

"What did you tell them?" she asked. Suddenly Laney's happiness was overshadowed by embarrassment.

"You're blushing, Laney," Michael said. "I've never seen you blush before."

"That's so personal," she said.

"I know," mumbled Michael. "But I told them just the same."

The two friends just sat there and didn't say a word. Michael's blond hair dipped over one eye as he rubbed his forehead.

"Oh brother," Laney groaned. "It looks as though I won't have much privacy after all. What did you tell them?"

"I told them it was soft and sensitive – a little different than other girls. That your lips sort of cause a tingling sensation."

Laney was very surprised to hear him mention other girls, but she didn't say anything about it. She felt a little jealous, but when he said her kiss was a bit special, she felt better.

She sighed and said, "What did they say?"

"They said they'd have to find out if that tingling was because of emotion or energy."

"What are you saying?" she yelled. "They aren't going to experiment with us kissing, are they?"

Michael blushed a deep red and said, "Yep. After you've been there a while, we'll be experimented with when we kiss each other. Don't get too upset, Laney. Do you realize how special you are to them?"

"To them?" she said. "What about to you?"

"You're my friend," said Michael. "My parents and I decided that I should visit you as often as I'm allowed."

"Well," Laney said. "I'm not going to kiss you in front of anybody!"

Laney brushed her hair from her eyes and stared at the floor. She thought of taking her glasses off but didn't. She knew she had to leave them on.

"Laney, don't be embarrassed. They'll want to know everything, so you may as well go along with them. Look at your other choices. It's either me or one of them."

At that they both laughed. Laney did feel a bit silly. But she could see that Michael was laughing away some of his nervousness, too.

"One thing about them, Laney," said Michael. "I don't think they'd ever ask you to do anything they didn't think you were ready to do. Remember, you're very special to them. They want you to be comfortable with your work there. So we will have time together like we do now, but we'll work, too."

"Oh great," she said. "Now our kissing and swimming will become work."

Laney's enthusiasm was disappearing. Now school seemed like a place worse than any other. She wanted to change her mind, but she knew deep inside that it would be the best place for her.

Finally, Michael said to her softly, "At first it'll be strange. But we'll both get used to it. Let's not let them get too experimental with us. If they do we'll just have to tell them."

Michael put his arm around Laney, and with his other hand, stroked her hair.

"My friend from outer space," he said softly. "Do you think you'll want to go back to where you're from once you figure that one out?"

"Only if you can come with me," she answered.

Michael left and Laney was alone. She knew she had a good friend in him. She was tired and still a little concerned about being in a school away from everyone. But the excitement was stronger than ever. Being from another planet didn't seem that bad after all.

Leaving for School

Michael was with Laney the day she packed. There was excitement throughout the house, and Laney was not only the cause of it but experienced most of it. She found out she'd have her own room that was quite bright. Dr. Bucci hadn't visited her since that day last week. She was actually looking forward to seeing him again, as well as meeting the others.

Michael was folding her denim jeans as he said, "Are you sure you'll be allowed to dress like this?"

"Sure," she replied. "They said it's just like high school."

"I hope you're right," he answered, "but just to be safe, you'd better take more dresses than just those two."

She packed two more dresses than she had intended and soon enough her parents and Phil were carrying her luggage out to the station wagon.

"Are you all set?" her father asked.

"Yes," Laney replied. "I'm ready to go to school and disintegrate whatever they wish."

"Just leave your glasses on during the drive," answered her father. "I'll need my steering wheel the whole way up and back."

They laughed, then they all walked out to the car. Michael said good-bye to her as she situated herself among the suitcases in the back seat.

Her father pulled out of the driveway and they started their drive to Laney's school. She didn't say anything but she was a little nervous again about living away from home in a school with other gifted people. Of course it was an exciting situation to be in, but how would she and the rest of them be treated? Would they be given everything they wanted? Would they be overworked? Were the rest of them temperamental? Did they look different from other students?

Laney was quiet for the first hour of the trip.

Finally, her mother remarked about her silence. Laney told her about her concerns. Her mother tried to reassure her. Although neither she nor Laney's father had met any of the other students, the staff had assured them that Laney's new schoolmates were just like any other high school kids. They would all have lunch breaks. They would have free periods, and dinner lasted two hours.

There were no group classes since she was much more gifted and special than the rest of them. They were telepathic or gifted in other ways, but Laney was from another planet with superhuman abilities. So during most classes Laney would work alone with one or two of the staff members.

Another hour passed, and off in the distance Laney could see a three-story brick building.

"That's the school," her father said.

They pulled into the driveway. Dr. Bucci was waiting there to greet them.

Arriving at School

"Hello, Laney," said Dr. Bucci. "You're right on time."

"Hello, Dr. Bucci," she responded. "Right on time for what?"

"For lunch, if you care to have it," he said. "Otherwise, after you put your things in your room, Dr. Henderson, our psychologist, will show you around the building. We even have a swimming pool."

Laney told him that she knew about the pool and she was eager to try it out. Her father and mother took her belongings to her room. It was painted mint green; the curtains and bedspread were yellow. The desk was very old, but lovely. When they finished they went back to the front of the building, where Dr. Bucci and Laney were still chatting.

They each gave her a kiss, and her mother said, "Good-bye, Sweetheart. We'll be back to visit you on parents' weekend. It's only a couple of months away."

"Call us if you need anything," said her father. "But they seem to be well-prepared for you here."

Her parents got in the car and drove down the road. Laney watched them until they disappeared into the valley.

"Come with me, Laney," said Dr. Bucci. You'll be able to meet some of the other students."

They went to the lunchroom. It was yellow and had small round tables, which sat four. Each table had green and yellow striped tablecloths. Dr. Bucci brought her to a table where a young black man sat.

"This is Tom," said Dr. Bucci. "Tom, this is Laney."

So this is Tom! Laney thought. *He doesn't seem very intriguing. But why is he sitting alone?* Other students walked by and said "hi," but Tom would only nod.

Tom looked up and said, "I feel I know you from somewhere."

"Thank you," said Laney. "But we've never met. At least to my re-collection we haven't."

Tom smiled and pulled the chair out for her to sit down. She sat and said, "I'm really not very hungry. May I just go to my room?" she asked Dr. Bucci. *Tom really is intriguing,* she thought.

"Of course," said Dr. Bucci. "I'll give you an hour or so. Then Dr. Henderson will be by. You'll meet the rest of the staff over the next couple of days. We don't want you to feel rushed in any way."

As Laney got up, Tom said, "I'm certain I know you from somewhere else. Perhaps we can talk later – after dinner."

His brown eyes glowed almost as much as the stones on the box her father had given her.

"I'd like that," she replied, almost as though she was in a trance. "See you then."

Dr. Bucci walked her to her room. "Tom is really a mystery student," he told her. "He came to us just a few days ago and seems to be looking for something – or someone. Perhaps you can help us out with him. He hasn't taken to anyone the way he has taken to you."

Laney didn't know what to say. Tom seemed very nice, but she felt there was something mysterious about him, too. She couldn't wait until after dinner.

Settling In

Laney went into her room and started to unpack. She was still thinking about Tom. She couldn't understand why she was so fascinated by him, but she wanted to talk to him more. As she was putting away her clothes, there was a knock at the door. It was a young staff member. She knew that because he was wearing a tie.

"Hello, Laney. I'm Dr. Henderson."

"You're the psychologist," she replied.

"That's right," he said. "I've come to show you around the school."

"Okay," she said. Laney put the last unpacked suitcase on the bed.

Dr. Henderson seemed very young to Laney. He had a neat beard and moustache, and was very friendly. He told her they would go to her own special classroom first. She wanted to ask him about Tom, but she didn't. She wanted to go to the source himself.

They walked downstairs to a brightly lit corridor, then stepped into a small room, which only had two chairs and a desk. On the desk was a machine with a strip of paper coming out of it.

Attached to the machine were several wires that had electrodes at the end of each.

"This is your classroom," Dr. Henderson said. "This machine is an electroencephalograph, or EEG for short. It is used to record your brain waves. These electrodes will be attached to your head. Don't worry, they won't hurt a bit."

"Will you always be using the EEG when we work together?" Laney asked.

"Not always," he replied. "Sometimes we will meet in your room. I'll be giving you tests and trying to help you remember where you're from. I may even hypnotize you if you want me to, or if we think you need it."

Laney sat in the chair and touched the electrodes. They didn't pinch, and Dr. Henderson told her he would use a cream to attach them and she wouldn't feel anything but the cream.

"When can I go for a swim?" Laney asked. "Although I've never been in a pool without Michael, I'm a good swimmer."

"A good swimmer!" exclaimed Dr. Henderson. "You were a mermaid when your father found you, remember?"

"No, I don't," she answered. She still couldn't believe that part.

"Well, we were hoping you'd ask about swimming. You can go this afternoon if you want to. But we'll want Dr. Black with us when you do."

"Who is Dr. Black?" Laney asked.

"She's our staff physician. If you do what we think you'll do, we'll want her with us."

"What do you think I'll do – turn into a mermaid?" asked Laney teasingly.

"Precisely!" said Dr. Henderson. "We'll see you at the pool at three o'clock."

Laney went back to her room. She was very excited. She didn't feel like unpacking, but knew she had to do something with all her energy. It was only two o'clock!

She unpacked the last suitcase and put it in her closet. It was about two-thirty when she put on her navy blue bathing suit and her robe. She was ready for her swim. A knock came at her door.

"Who's there?" she asked.

"Dr. Black," a female voice responded.

She opened the door and a tall blond woman in a white lab coat entered her room. "All ready for your swim, I see," she said.

"Yes, Dr. Black. I am," Laney answered.

"Please just let me take your pulse, blood pressure and temperature before you go in the water. I want to see if they change when you do."

"So you're convinced I'll turn into a mermaid, too?" Laney asked.

"Shhhh," she said with a smile on her face. She listened to Laney's heartbeat with her stethoscope. Then they walked to the indoor pool together.

At the Pool

When they got to the pool, Dr. Bucci and Dr. Henderson were waiting.

"We're just here to observe," said Dr. Henderson. "Dr. Black will work with you when you get out of the water."

Laney tested the water with her foot and found that the temperature was fine. She dove in. She felt her legs get closer together as she kicked in the water. Even without Michael, she was able to swim very fast. Then she heard Dr. Henderson shout, "Look! She's turning into a mermaid! Her hair is getting longer and lighter. Look at that tail fin. See how the scales shimmer in the light. What speed! She could probably win against the world's top swimmers!"

At last, Laney swam at the speed she had never reached before. She was indeed a mermaid.

She swam back and forth in the pool. She looked graceful and sleek. Her green scales shimmered and glowed in the water. She no longer had a human form, but that didn't matter. She was content and calm in the water, as though she had always belonged there. Then she heard Dr. Bucci say, "Come out of the water, Laney."

She didn't want to, but she saw the expression on his face. He looked worried.

She got out of the water and looked at herself. She was beautiful. Dr. Black went over to her and took her pulse, blood pressure and temperature.

"Absolutely no change," she said as she took the thermometer out of Laney's mouth.

"Isn't she magnificent?" asked Dr. Henderson. "But how does she get back to human form?"

Laney flapped her tail fin with delight.

"I don't know," said Dr. Bucci. "That's what I'm worried about."

There's no need to worry," Laney said to Dr. Bucci. "I know how."

She leaned against the wall and thought about how she looked in her human form. In seconds she was in that shape once again. She put her glasses back on.

After a couple of moments, she stood up. The doctors were all huddled around her. They looked serious and bewildered.

"Why do you all look so confused?" Laney asked.

"You looked so beautiful, so comfortable, as though that's the way you should be," said Dr. Henderson. "We don't know if we should keep you in your human form or let you remain a mermaid while you're here."

"I'm comfortable as both," Laney said to them all. "Leave me as a human, but let me swim every day."

They agreed. As Laney put her robe on, Dr. Black asked, "Do you feel tired?"

"No," Laney said. "I feel perfectly relaxed."

"Then perhaps we should go to your room and talk, Laney. This may be a good time to look into your past," said Dr. Henderson.

They walked to her room together and talked about any memory she had about being a mermaid. She told him that she could remember just a little. That she knew the moment she was in the water she was at peace there.

"That must mean there's plenty of water on the planet from which you came," said Dr. Henderson.

"Or that my people feel safer in the water," responded Laney.

Now she even talked as though she was from another planet. She told him she had a strange feeling that her planet may have been in jeopardy. They both agreed that may be nothing but a guess.

They talked until about five o'clock, and Dr. Henderson asked if she wanted to have dinner in the cafeteria or in her room. Laney said her room. She didn't feel like being with people just yet. That was quite an experience for her. He said he would have her dinner sent up directly and thanked her for getting to work so soon. Laney said he was welcome, and he left to order her dinner. She sat on the bed and wanted to call her parents, but then she remembered they already knew. That's how they had found her eight years ago.

Laney took a nap. A knock at her door woke her up.

"Who is it?"

"Tom."

She opened the door and it was the boy she had seen in the cafeteria earlier in the day.

"May I come in?" he asked.

"Of course," she answered.

Tom's News

"Let me get right to the point," Tom said. "I'm not from this Earth, either. I am Kertar, from the planet Amis."

"Don't kid about that, Tom."

"If you think I'm kidding, watch this," he said. At that, silver, feather-like lights appeared around him. "This is what I really look like," he said in a much deeper voice. "Just as you take the shape of a mermaid in the water, I look like this on my planet…and yours."

"The human-like figure!" Laney exclaimed. "I saw it twice while I was disintegrating objects for Dr. Bucci!" Laney was thrilled.

"I was trying to reach you then, but you disintegrated the objects too fast," Kertar continued. "Now I need some of your power to take back to your planet – the planet Thrae."

"'Thrae.' That's almost Earth spelled backwards," said Laney. "Is that where I'm from?"

"Yes," said Kertar, now back in human form. "The planet Thrae is being attacked by the Garnots. You were sent to Earth eight Earth-years ago by your parents to keep your power pure and untouched, so that now you could give some of it to someone like me. There is no need for you to return to Thrae – yet. Just give me some of your power."

"How?" Laney asked. "But wait. Before I do, I want Dr. Bucci and Dr. Henderson to be here."

"There is no time," Kertar answered. There was urgency in his voice.

"Then we'll make time," Laney said. "They need to know about this."

"Okay, call them in," Kertar said. "But we don't have any time to waste."

She ran to the staff office and found Dr. Bucci. As they both raced back to her room, they saw Dr. Henderson carrying her dinner tray. As soon as Dr. Henderson saw them together he said, "Go ahead, I'll catch up." Dr. Bucci asked Laney to bring Kertar to her classroom, so Dr. Henderson could set up the EEG. He wanted to record her brain waves as she gave Kertar some of her power.

Once Laney and Kertar arrived in her classroom, Dr. Henderson and Dr. Black came rushing in. Dr. Henderson attached the electrodes to Laney's head.

What do I do?" Laney asked Kertar.

"Just take off your glasses and stare into my eyes."

"Okay," she said, "but won't you be disintegrated?"

"No," he Kertar. "Just stare."

She stared into his eyes and within seconds he transformed. His eyes pulsated a green light, and he began to glow. He spoke: "Thrae is several galaxies away. When I'm finished here, I'll have enough energy to go back to Thrae and defeat the Garnots."

"When do I stop staring?" Laney asked.

"When I turn into a ray of green light," he answered.

"Are you getting tired?" Dr. Bucci asked Laney. "Your brain waves are still uniform," Dr. Henderson said, as he watched the strip of paper come from the machine.

"She has the strength of twelve armies," said Kertar, who was now aglow with green light.

"I don't feel tired," Laney said. "But I am just as amazed as you are."

A few more minutes passed and Kertar was still glowing.

"We'll have to stop," he said. "There's not enough energy here." He looked disappointed. The green glow was disappearing.

"What do you mean?" Laney asked.

"You concentrate energy," replied Kertar, who now looked human again. "You take the energy that's around you and put it into things. Or, when you disintegrate things, you take the energy away. The energy goes through you so it's always changed into something else. There isn't enough electricity in this building for you to give me the power I need."

"So, I need a bigger power source," Laney responded.

"That's right, Laney," said Kertar. "And what's the biggest power source this Earth has?"

"The sun!" interjected Dr. Bucci.

"That's right," Kertar answered.

"So tomorrow," said Dr. Henderson, "you'll go outdoors."

"Precisely," said Kertar. "Just as the sun comes up would be the best time."

"Okay," said Dr. Bucci. "Tonight Dr. Black, Dr. Henderson and I will work with Kertar, and tomorrow we can watch Laney finish the job."

"That's okay with me," Laney said.

"Me too," said Kertar. "Laney should rest tonight, but I know all of you have things you want to talk to me about."

The doctors and Kertar left the room and went into another classroom. Laney went back to her quarters. The dinner on her tray was cold, so she decided to go to the dining room to have a bite to eat.

In the Dining Room

When she got to the dining room, Laney was approached by a girl with brown hair. "Hi. I'm Nancy," she said with a smile. "Why don't you come to our table to eat?" She pointed to where she was sitting with two other girls and a boy.

"Sure," Laney said, and she took her tray over to the table.

Nancy introduced the two other girls as Lisa and Erin and the boy as Charles. They all said hello and ate their meals quietly.

Afterwards, Nancy asked, "How do you like it here, Laney?"

"So far, so good," Laney answered. She wanted to tell them about what had happened that day, so soon after her arrival. She was about to tell them, but Charles interrupted her thoughts.

"What's your gift?" he asked.

"Now Charles," said Lisa. "You know you're not supposed to ask that."

Laney was glad she didn't say anything after all. She didn't understand why, but now she knew that she couldn't discuss her abilities.

"What gift?" she said. "And why shouldn't he ask about it?"

"Your gift," said Lisa, "is the reason you're in this school. We're not supposed to ask about it because it's up for investigation here. It's not supposed to be bragged about. Some kids say they have a gift, but it takes them a long time to prove it. Some never prove it at all."

"Oh, come on, Lisa," retorted Charles. "Let's see why Laney is here."

"You don't have to say anything, Laney," said Nancy. "Charles is one of the ones who hasn't proved anything yet. He's just being a royal neb-nose."

Charles looked angry. He stood up and slammed his fist on the table. "Well, I will!" shouted Charles. "Just you wait and see. I'll show all of you!"

At that, Charles left the table. Everyone sat quietly for a moment, then Erin, who hadn't said anything so far, said, "He's too much of a hothead."

They could all see that, but they were still a little upset over Charles's outburst.

"Let's go to my room and talk some more," said Lisa.

"I can't," said Nancy. "I'm supposed to get plenty of rest tonight."

"I'd like that," Laney said, "for a little while. How about you, Erin?"

"Okay," said Erin. "Let's go."

Nancy got up from the table, said good night and walked away. Laney really wanted to talk to her newfound friends about what had happened and was happy to go with them. She really was enjoying her day.

The three girls got up together, put their trays in the bin and walked to Lisa's room. They sat on the bed and Laney asked, "How long have you been here, Erin?"

"I'm going on my second year," Erin answered.

"How about you, Lisa?" Laney turned to her.

"Oh, I'm going on my third year."

"How do you both like it?"

"I like it a lot," said Erin. "I'm not treated as anything special here."

Then Erin put her eyes down and started to pull a thread out of the bedspread. She seemed so shy.

"What do you mean?" Laney questioned.

"Erin was brought up as though she was a very special girl," said Lisa. "She wasn't allowed to have any real friends or anything, because her parents wanted to protect her and keep her for the specialists. That's why she's so shy. Were you brought up that way, Laney?"

"Oh no," Laney said. "I just found out about my powers recently."

Erin raised her eyes and mumbled, "You're lucky."

"You don't have to be shy with me, Erin," said Laney. "Maybe between the two of us we'll get you away from that shyness." Laney winked at Lisa.

"I doubt it," said Lisa. "I've tried for a whole year."

"Well, maybe Laney can help," said Erin. "I like you, Lisa, but there's something really special about Laney."

They laughed and talked in Lisa's room until about nine o'clock. Then there was a flickering of the lights.

"What was that?" Laney asked.

"That means we all have to be in our own rooms by nine-thirty. At ten o'clock we should be in bed."

"Well, it is getting late," said Erin.

"Yes, it is," Laney responded. "I'd better get some sleep. Thanks for the talk, and I hope to see the two of you at breakfast."

"You will," said Erin.

"Right," said Lisa.

Laney left the girls and went back to her room. She didn't think ten o'clock was an unreasonable hour, but she had to remind herself to ask about the weekends. It had been an exciting, surprising and fun day. Laney was happy. She thought for a moment to call her parents, but by nine-thirty she fell fast asleep.

Laney, the Sun and Kertar

The next morning, Laney was awake at six. By six-thirty, there was a knock at her door. It was Dr. Bucci.

"All ready?" he asked her.

"Yes," she answered, "but I feel a little nervous." This was her first morning in school and she was feeling a bit shy herself.

"There's nothing to be nervous about," he told her. "We learned a lot about you last night from Kertar."

Laney and Dr. Bucci walked slowly down the corridor. Laney had everything, and nothing, to say. This was all very new to her.

They went outside, and it seemed that the ever-giving sun was shining brighter than ever. It rose high and yellow above the poplar trees behind the school. Kertar came out with Dr. Henderson and Dr. Black.

"Now take your glasses off and stare into my eyes like you did last night," said Kertar to Laney. "Think about how warm and strong the sun is."

She took off her glasses and stared into his eyes. In just a minute or two, Kertar transformed himself, and began to glow. Red and yellow flames appeared around him.

Laney was overwhelmed but kept staring. The flames got higher and brighter. Kertar kept staring back. Then, about a minute later, he turned into a twenty-foot pillar of green light and went soaring into the sky. No rocket launch was ever as magnificent.

"Are you all right?" asked Dr. Black. "You seem a little pale."

"I'm fine," said Laney. "But I wish he could have told me more about why I was sent here."

But Drs. Henderson and Black had recorded their conversations with Kertar. Laney would be allowed to listen to them.

"Well, Laney, you've wasted no time since you arrived. What's next?" asked Dr. Bucci with a smile.

"I don't know," she replied. She was feeling quite good about herself. What an accomplishment!

"We learned quite a bit about you from Kertar," Dr. Bucci said.

"That's right," said Dr. Henderson. He patted Laney on the back.

"We all have our work with you cut out for us," said Dr. Black.

"And that will give us all plenty to work with," sighed Dr. Bucci. "We didn't realize what we had bargained for, bringing you here." He just shook his head and grinned. Obviously Laney wasn't the only one who was awestruck.

"At least you have a better idea of what it will be like to work with us," said Dr. Henderson. "Disintegrating is nothing compared to what you are capable of."

"I hope everything is all right on my planet," Laney finally said. "Kertar never would have come here if it weren't an emergency, right?"

"Yes," said Dr. Black, "but he knows where you are if he needs more help."

The doctors all knew why he had come.

"Well, I hope you're right," Laney said softly. "It's not easy trying to help the people of a planet you don't even remember."

"Well, Laney," said Dr. Bucci, "maybe you'll have to return to Thrae yourself someday."

"If I find out how," she said with tears in her eyes.

"Oh, you will," said Dr. Henderson as he put his arm around her. "You will."

Judith Galardi

Part II

Judith Galardi

What Next?

Laney knew she had a lot of work ahead of her, but wasn't sure where to begin. Her powers, the Garnots, Thrae in danger – all seemed to be a great deal to handle at once. She sat at her desk and looked over the rolling green hills and the pond below. Her planet, like Earth, was three-quarters covered with water. She'd have to find a way back and a way to save Thrae. Dr. Bucci said he'd help – actually she was sure they all would – but she was determined to figure out as much as she could on her own.

The image of Kertar was on her mind too. He seemed to have enough power to conquer any army but now she wasn't sure. Perhaps he didn't even make it to Thrae. Perhaps the Garnots were too powerful for him. Perhaps he was too late. Tears formed in her eyes. Although it was only seven p.m., she felt tired. She put her head down and prayed. After her prayer, she fell asleep.

Dr. Henderson's knock at the door woke her up. It was seven-thirty. "Good morning again, Laney," he shouted. "Time for breakfast if you're interested."

Leaning back in her chair, she answered: "Wait. I want breakfast, but I need to talk to you."

She opened the door. Dr. Henderson was grinning broadly. He clapped his hands together once and asked how the "power hitter" was. Laney told him her worries about Kertar, Thrae, her own powers. She sat at her desk and asked him how she could get back to Thrae if no one knew where it was.

"Kertar will be back," replied Dr. Henderson.

"How can you be sure? Wonder if –," stammered Laney.

"Laney, don't be so unsure of yourself, or Kertar. We're convinced he'll be back. Later this morning we'll meet with you and we'll explain it. I understand your worries, but believe me, you have no reason to worry. Besides, worrying never solves anything. It only drains your energy. So just be calm. You'll need all the strength you can get this afternoon. Speaking of strength, why don't you go have some breakfast? It'll give you a chance to relax with the rest of the students." He patted her on the back.

She rested her head in her hand and sighed. How she wished she understood more. But she trusted Dr. Henderson, so she just smiled, said, "see you later," and left for the dining room. As she walked down the hall she ran into Lisa.

"Good morning," said Lisa. "Did you sleep well?"

Laney laughed to herself and told Lisa that she had a very pleasant sleep. Lisa started to talk fast and practically without hesitation about the classes she had ahead of her that day. Laney kept staring at her trying to keep up with everything she was saying.

Lisa stopped in mid-sentence and said, "You're not usually very active in the morning, are you?"

Laney laughed and asked if it showed. Lisa said: "Well, yeah. But I love to talk. So if it's okay with you, I'll keep going, but I'll try to slow it down."

They stepped into the dining room and got in line. There were about fifteen students ahead of them and about twenty-five already seated. Lisa explained that there were sixty-eight students in the school and that they had come from all over the world. Many of them were gifted with extrasensory perception, or esp, and they could do things such as tell you the symbol on the card you were holding, even if they were blindfolded. Some could even tell you what color the symbol was.

Laney was fascinated. She imagined herself trying to do that. Then she remembered that if she took her glasses off, she'd disintegrate the card rather than just see through it. She wondered, *could I be taught how to do that? Not disintegrate something, but just see through it?* Then she remembered what she had been told last night and said: "Ahhh, Lisa. No discussing powers, right?"

Lisa grinned and said, "Well, that's true. But I'm just talking about it in general. And I'm not talking about mine, or yours."

"Li-sa," Laney said. Lisa nodded her head and ordered her food.

The food looked good — muffins, cereal, eggs, pancakes, juices, bacon, yogurt, coffee and tea. Laney enjoyed being in line, asking for various things. It was very different from middle school, but all the same she thought about home.

She'd have finished breakfast by now. Phil would be clearing the table and she'd be loading the dishwasher.

Eileen would still be playing with her food and David would be sweeping the floor. *My Earth family,* she thought. *What fun we had, and I hope, will have.* She carried her tray to the table and sat down. Lisa, Nancy and Erin were already there. Charles was on his way over.

"Good morning, folks," said Laney. "Did you sleep well?"

Erin nodded and said: "Good morning. How was your sleep?"

"Fine," answered Laney.

"Good morning," said Nancy. "I'm not awake yet." She yawned and sipped her juice.

Charles dropped his tray on the table and said, "'Morning everyone."

The girls looked quickly at each other and shouted joyously together, "Good morning, Charles!"

Charles tried not to smile but did anyway. He sat down and sipped his tea. Surprisingly, Erin began to talk about her classes that day.

"I'll be trying my luck at telekinesis, you know, being able to move an object just by concentrating on it. Whoops, sorry. It's hard not to talk about school when you're there twenty-four hours a day, isn't it?"

They all agreed, even Charles.

The conversation turned to hobbies and extracurricular activities. Erin liked playing the flute and hiking. She wasn't allowed to participate in any really active sports because her parents didn't want her to get hurt. She hoped to go swimming sometime, though.

Nancy enjoyed tennis and listening to rock music. She asked Erin if she knew any rock and Erin said she didn't. Laney asked her if she could learn some. Erin hesitated a little and said sure. Charles said he liked swimming, but when Laney suggested that he teach Erin, he said: "No. That's why this place has a phys. ed. teacher. Erin doesn't need me."

He put his fork on his plate and dropped his head in his hand. Everyone except Erin became a little suspicious of his comment.

"What about you, Laney?" asked Nancy. "What do you like to do?"

"Oh, I like swimming and reading."

"What kind of books?" asked Erin.

"Adventure!" exclaimed Laney. "I like to read about exciting situations and faraway places."

"Actually," said Charles, "I like adventure stuff too. I like it when people big, strong, and mean get what they deserve from somebody nobody expects."

"I read a story like that once," said Erin. "There was this small town. I don't know where. Everyone in it except a young boy was controlled by some kind of evil mastermind who used sound waves to control people. The boy wasn't controlled because he was deaf. Eventually he figured things out, like a detective. He dismantled the machine and told his parents and friends. Then the town was freed and the mastermind was captured."

"Hmmmm," said Charles. "That sounds like a neat story. Could I borrow it?"

"Well, ahhh, you may come by my room, sort of after breakfast if you want," replied Erin.

"Oh, no. That's okay. I mean, maybe you can give it to me at lunch. That's if we're going to have lunch together."

"Yeah, we will," said Erin. "Won't we everybody?"

"Right," said Nancy, smiling.

Laney nodded and grinned. *Oh gosh*, she thought. *What have we here*?

Everyone got up, took their trays to the drop-off, and went to their various classes.

The Hypnotic Trance

Laney went to her room and waited. This was supposed to be her hypnosis morning, but she wasn't sure now. Not after what she had done earlier. Dr. Henderson walked in.

"Well, how was breakfast?"

"Oh fine," Laney answered. "Things are a lot different for me here. A whole lot different."

"In more ways than you ever thought, I'll bet," replied Dr. Henderson. "And it's going to be even more different this morning. Have you ever been hypnotized?"

"No. But I'll bet I'm about to be."

"Well, well – clairvoyant, too. When did that happen?"

They laughed.

Dr. Henderson continued. "There's really nothing to hypnosis. It's just a very relaxed state that one goes into. The more relaxed you are, the more likely it is that you'll be able to remember things that certain matters tend to make one forget. It's painless and most people find it to be very pleasant. Any questions?"

"Yeah," said Laney, "what if it doesn't work? I mean, what if I can't remember anything?"

"Maybe it won't work this time. If it doesn't, we'll try again. In a week or so I hope to have you to the point where you'll be able to hypnotize yourself. Of course, you'll only need to use it here, but – you never know. Ready?"

Laney answered yes and they began. Dr. Henderson told her to sit in the most comfortable position she could. She sat straight up in the chair with her feet on the floor and her arms, from the elbows down to her fingertips, resting gently on the arms of the chair. She closed her eyes.

"Oh, don't close your eyes, at least not yet," said Dr. Henderson. "I'm going to ask you to do something for me first. Look straight ahead at that picture on the wall. Don't squint, and whatever you do, don't take off your glasses. Just look at the picture and concentrate on one small part of it that appeals to you. Then calmly listen to my voice."

He started to count backwards from ten. He told Laney to imagine herself floating alone in the ocean. No great waves, nothing to annoy, frighten, or in any way upset the peaceful state she was in. Then he told her to close her eyes.

"The water is a normal, gentle place for you, Laney. You've been there before – several years ago, in fact. You know this place. You even know the sky. You know this place very well."

Laney let the water hug her – the warm water she had known so well. She felt safe. She felt sure. She was at home.

Suddenly a large dome appeared in the distance; a crystal dome that glittered and sparkled in the sun-light. Laney swam toward it. As she approached it she was able to find a space to go into it. The moment she entered, her tail fin disappeared and her legs appeared. She walked down a long hallway. Pictures lined the walls – pictures of the sea, the sky, underwater, mer-people. She came to a room.

As she entered, she saw a woman with brown curly hair and a long gold dress. The woman radiated a soft golden light all around her. She smiled at Laney and at once Laney had a feeling that she knew this woman from somewhere, somehow.

"Who are you?" asked Laney, feeling drawn in by the aura of the woman.

"I'm sorry you don't recognize me," said the woman. "Maybe it has been too long after all. I've been trying to reach you for a long time, but it appears that being on Earth for so long has somehow weakened the communicative powers between us. I'm Diana-Mer. I'm your mother on Thrae."

Laney began to shout, "No! No!" Then she heard Dr. Henderson say, "Laney, Laney, it's okay. Relax. Start to concentrate on your breathing. Slowly, slowly, breathe in and out. That's it." Laney slowly and deliberately breathed in and out. She was calmer.

Then Dr. Henderson said, "As I count to ten, you will open your eyes, then look around the room slowly. Don't move suddenly and please don't try to get up until we've had a couple of minutes to talk."

"One, two, three...."

Laney opened her eyes and looked straight ahead.

"Four, five...."

Laney looked around the room and saw Dr. Henderson. She did not speak.

"Six, seven, eight...."

She stretched her head and neck from side to side and stretched her arms and legs out in front of her.

"Nine, ten."

She said, "I don't want to do that again. Please!"

"Just take it easy," said Dr. Henderson. "Can you tell me what you saw?"

"No. Just don't ask me to do that again. And don't ask me any questions about it."

Dr. Henderson was concerned about Laney's frightened reaction. He tried to get her to talk but she refused. She just kept asking him to leave her alone for awhile. He said okay, but that he'd be back in fifteen minutes. He asked her if she thought she'd be able to talk then. After thinking for a couple of minutes she said, "I'll try."

She sat alone. *My mother,* she thought. *How could she have sent me here without an explanation? She said we haven't been able to communicate. Why is she trying now? Is she in some kind of danger, or is she trying to say good-bye for good? I can't even remember her. Does she still love me?*

Laney sighed and closed her eyes. She just wanted to rest and let her mind wander. But it wouldn't. Her thoughts kept going back to her Thrae mother with the aura that seemed to be drawing Laney back. Dr. Henderson returned to the room.

"Well," he said. "It sounded like you were having quite a time of it, or shall I say, quite a scare."

"I saw my mother."

"You mean your Earth mother?"

"No, Diana-Mer. My Thrae mother."

"And that scared you?"

"Yes."

"Did she say something to scare you?"

"Not exactly."

"Did she look scary?"

"No."

"What, then?"

"What does she want with me?"

"She's your mother."

"Since when?"

"Since you were born."

"She dumped me!"

"Did she? Kertar said you were sent here – not dumped – to protect you and to keep your powers pure. Remember?"

"Yeah, but she…."

"She what?"

"She never talked to me until now!"

"Did she say why?"

"Well, ahhh, she said our communication powers had weakened, or something like that."

"So she has been trying."

"So."

"So? Feeling a little betrayed, are you?"

"I didn't say that."

"You didn't?"

"Not exactly."

"What else did she say?"

"Nothing."

"Did you speak to her?"

"No. I broke loose."

"It could be that the hypnosis allowed you to be close enough for your mother to reach you for the first time since you've been here."

"Then why did she dump me?"

"Why don't you ask her?"

Laney slumped back in her chair and looked out the window. She longed for the not-so-olden days when she had a normal family life in a normal house. Now she was troubled down to her very soul. She noticed a bluebird on a branch outside the window. It arched its back and stretched its wings and threw its chest forward. It pecked at the branch for a moment, as though it was sending some kind of coded message, then brushed both sides of its beak on the branch. It nodded to Laney as if to say, "Everything's okay." Another bluebird, a slightly larger one, flew to the tree and landed on a higher branch. The first bird went to that branch and they both quietly looked toward the sun. The larger one seemed to lean on the other.

"Let's try the hypnosis again," she said. "But not now. Tomorrow."

"Okay," said Dr. Henderson. "It's time to break for lunch anyway. We'll do it tomorrow." He went to the door, turned and said: "Laney, you're one of the most courageous people I've ever met. Both of your mothers – and fathers – should be proud." He walked out and closed the door behind him.

She looked out the window at the two bluebirds. They were still sitting together. The larger one looked over its shoulder at her. It broke into song, the smaller one did the same, then they both took off.

She felt better now. A message, she thought. Stick to my mother – my Thrae mother. We'll be okay together from now on. She decided to go for a walk before her appointment at the pool. She was very relieved. What she didn't notice was that after the two birds flew together for a couple of minutes, they separated – each going its own way.

At the Pool

Dr. Bucci was waiting for Laney. Laney had decided that today she would try to set a new speed record. Of course, she hadn't informed the staff of that decision so what was about to happen would be a new experience for all of them, especially Laney.

She got into the water and began to swim. Her hair grew longer, she grew fins. She swam faster. Her scales turned from green to silver, her body became more elongated. Dr. Bucci began to yell to her to slow down, but she couldn't hear anything.

The water began to glow a bright green. Laney's body became sleek. She was no longer swimming the breast stroke, but gliding through the water effortlessly. She was no longer aware of being in a pool, or in the school, or with Dr. Bucci. It was as if she had transported to a new body in a new body of water.

Suddenly, the pool became still. Dr. Bucci called for Laney but she had disappeared. He went to get the other members of the staff. This was one skill none of them knew she had.

Laney transformed back into her mermaid shape. The water around her was a pale peach color, and it was much warmer than earlier. It was much deeper too, so deep that she could barely see the bottom. At the bottom were what looked like pillars and statues, but she figured she had to be mistaken. The bottom of the pool was white tile, and at its deepest point it was ten feet. She thought she was seeing things, that swimming so fast had made her a little light-headed. She lifted her head above water to ask Dr. Bucci what time she had made; she was excited about what might have been her new speed record. Racing added a whole new area of promise.

When she raised her head she saw an enormous crystal dome about three hundred yards away. She couldn't make out what was inside it. It looked like cubicles made of glass of different colors, but she wasn't sure. She debated whether or not to swim closer when suddenly a wave overtook her and forced her downward. The water surged around her and she tumbled down, tossed like a toy boat from side to side. Finally she re-gained control and found herself several feet below the surface. She opened her eyes and couldn't see very much since the water around her had become murky. Suddenly a figure appeared coming toward her. It looked like a large fish – maybe six feet long. She swam rapidly toward the surface, but the fish was getting closer and closer. She made it to the surface and was about to scream when the fish surfaced, too. It was not a fish at all, but a mer-man!

"Come with me," he said to her. "I'll take you where it's safe."

Laney shook her head, not having given it any thought. She looked ahead at the dome again. Suddenly she remembered – the dome in hypnosis! Could it possibly be?

"Laney," said the mer-man. "I'm a friend of yours from a long time ago. I can't explain now, except to say that you're not safe here. Come with me."

Suddenly Laney remembered the dome she saw during her hypnosis. She believed him. She knew she was on Thrae.

Okay, she thought. *I know where I am now.*

"We'll swim over to that life-space. We'll be able to talk there," he said.

They swam quietly together. Laney noticed that there was nothing else around but the dome – rather, the life-space. She looked down into the water again. There were more pillars and statues, but she still couldn't make out any detail. In fact, it was harder to see. The water was getting deeper, not more shallow. She looked at her companion. Unlike her, his scales were a grayish-blue and his tail fin wasn't as wide as hers, yet he was able to swim right along with her. She wondered if she had developed differently because she had spent so much time on Earth.

When they got within a few feet of the life-space, she could see that a small section of the bottom of it was open and the rest was crystal. Her companion swam right through the opening and waved for Laney to do the same. When she got through, he was standing with his hand extended down to her. He helped her onto the platform.

As soon as she got out of the water she looked around. There were different-colored glass cubicles around her, each one about twelve feet by twelve feet. There were people – or at least they looked like people – inside the cubicles looking out their windows into the water. Some people were looking at computer terminals; others were holding compasses and other instruments.

"Are they people or are they from Thrae?" she asked her companion.

"People from Thrae are people, but we call ourselves Thraeans," he replied. "My name is Ostagus, I've been a friend of yours, your family, since before you were born. I was one of the ones who helped you get to Earth."

"How?"

"The same way you got back here."

"Thanks. That explains everything."

"I'll explain, I promise. There are a few of us up here who have a lot of explaining to do."

Finally, thought Laney, things may begin to make sense.

The Attack

At that moment, a huge wave smashed up against the wall of the life-space. The Thraeans were thrown about the corridors and their cubicles. Ostagus grabbed Laney and pulled her to the floor, protecting her with his body. Furniture was flying. Glass crashed down around them. People huddled in the doorways.

After a couple of moments the gyrating stopped. Everyone who was able got up and went to help others who couldn't. Ostagus helped Laney to her feet.

"Are you all right?" he asked Laney.

"Yeah," she replied. "Are you?"

He assured her he was fine as he brushed glass from his hair. Someone walked by them, patting him on his back and saying: "At last you brought her back. We hope it's not too late."

A voice was heard throughout the life-space saying: "The damage was minor. Continue assisting your friends. Repeat. The damage was minor. Please assist your friends."

"What was that?" she asked. "A tidal wave?"

"Not quite, Laney, I can't explain now. We need to help our friends. Do you feel up to it?"

"Sure," said Laney. "Just tell me what to do."

"That's the spirit," he said, squeezing her shoulder. "That's just the attitude we're looking for."

They walked over to a man who was lying on the floor. He had a cut on his forehead, but he was not bleeding.

"We'd better see to him right away," Ostagus said.

"Why?" asked Laney. "He isn't even bleeding."

"That's why we have to help him," said Ostagus. "He's frozen."

Laney touched the man's arm. It was ice cold. His skin was transparent. She could see his blood vessels; there were blue crystals suspended in them. His eyes were shut; there were icicles on them.

"What do we do?" she asked.

"We need to find two volunteers who will get into a sleeve with him."

Two Threans came by. One of them said: "We'll be glad to do it, Ostagus. Our lives are his."

"I'll get the sleeve," said the other. "There's one in my cubicle."

Ostagus and the volunteers gently picked up the man and carried him into the cubicle. One of them walked over to a shelf and picked up something made of silver-colored metallic cloth. The man shook it out; it was like a large sleeping bag. He opened it and the three of them placed the frozen man in the middle, then the two volunteers lay on either side of him.

Ostagus closed the bag, sealed it up one side and said to Laney, "This may take a while. This is one of the worst cases of freezing we've seen yet."

"We'll do our best," said one of the men. "We'll start concentrating now."

The volunteers closed their eyes and a green glow appeared and surrounded the sleeve. They became still.

"Let's go," Ostagus said to Laney. "There may be others who need us. I do believe our friend is going to make it."

"Are you a doctor?" she asked him.

"In a way," he answered. "Inside each of us is the cure. We just have to be in touch with it at the right time."

"That glow — I've seen that glow before."

"Of course you have," he answered. "All Thraeans have it."

"Then why didn't you suggest that I get into the sleeve, too?"

"Because you must save your power. It's vital to us now."

"Is it the Garnots?"

"Yes."

"Who are they?"

"I'll tell you about them later. Now we must help put this life-space back together."

The two walked down the corridor. There was broken glass everywhere. There were also sleeves everywhere. Men and women were in them. It was always the same; the frozen person in the middle, the volunteers on either side and a green glow surrounding them all. They came to a large room. There were people sitting on the floor with shawls draped over their shoulders that looked like the same material as the sleeves. The green glow was everywhere.

The crisis seems to be over for now," Ostagus said. "Everyone is in good color-light."

"May I walk around the room?" she asked.

"Certainly," he said. "But don't talk to anyone. They are thriving off the silence."

Laney tiptoed around the room. *The Thraeans look very human,* she thought. It didn't occur to her that humans looked very Thraean. All of them had their eyes closed and were breathing in unison. Through the green glow she could see their flesh; it had a bluish tint that faded even as she watched. There was a large crystal pyramid hanging from the ceiling. There were various colors flashing inside. A voice came from it.

"Soon all will be back to normal, my friends. Just take in the silence. Seventeen of us have been revived in the sleeves, ten more are showing promise. Five are seriously ill. Concentrate on the five. Think of the petals of the catekit flower, how the five of them together produce so much beauty. If one petal is taken away, only one, the whole flower dies. Imagine the flower intact. Build a catekit, one petal at a time. Feel its smooth petal between your fingers, smell the aroma. Sense the tingles it sends through your finger-tips as you place it on the stem. Now pick up the next petal, slowly,

slowly blow on it first – the first breath of life for it. Now place it on the stem. Take the next petal –."

As the voice directed, each person made the motions, although there were no petals or flowers in their hands. By watching them, Laney could imagine them piecing the flower together.

They got to the fifth petal and the voice said, "The last, the crowning glory of the catekit. Put it to your lips, then place it as the top petal."

Every person was holding his or her imaginary – or was it imaginary? – flower and placed the petal at the top. Then they all sighed and went back to their unified breathing.

"The five have come back to us. Congratulations my dear friends, the five have come back. You may come back now, too. Thank you, you've done wonderful work."

The Thraeans slowly opened their eyes and began hugging each other, shaking each other's hand; some bowed to each other. They were smiling, some were laughing and some just had very peaceful looks on their faces. Their flesh was all completely normal, and the green glow had disappeared. Laney walked back to Ostagus.

"They saved the lives of the five, just by thinking about the flower!" Laney exclaimed.

"Not just thinking, but by actually placing the life of each person in each petal. The last person was the sickest, that's why he was given the place of the top petal."

"But if any of the petals failed they all would have died," said Laney. "They should have put the sickest one on first; he would have become stronger by being on the stem longer."

"Not quite. The petals give life to the stem, not vice versa. Also, by putting the less sick on first, they become well, so they can will the sickest one well, too. Even the sick who became well gave their strength to the sickest."

"Couldn't they have become sick again?"

"No, not this time. Once one is unfrozen, one remains unfrozen until the next— I mean—."

"The next what?"

"I can't tell you now. There's someone you must see first."

Ostagus put his arm around her and they walked toward the back of the hall. People were still embracing and laughing, nodding to them as they passed. The green glow was practically gone from everyone with the exception of a couple of people. They approached one of them.

He turned to them and said: "Hi, Laney. Nice to see you on this planet for a change."

"Kertar!" she exclaimed. "How are you? How did you get here? You're safe!"

"Fine. You sent me. You're right," he said. "I hope I answered your questions satisfactorily."

They all laughed and Laney felt a little more comfortable. She put her hand on his shoulder and said: "I wondered about you, after that spectacular exit. How long did it take you to get here?"

"I got here as quickly as you sent me."

"That's not much of an answer."

"We aren't in the same time frame as you're trying to put us in. How long did it take you to get here?"

"A few minutes, ahhhh, seconds. Well, maybe it was somewhere around...."

"Somewhere around a time you can't quantify," said Kertar. "We don't use time the way one uses it on Earth. In fact, we don't use time at all. Time uses us."

"What?"

"We become a part of the time element. We become time. Time then becomes us and we behave accordingly."

"Right," answered Laney. "It's quite clear to me now."

"Think of it this way," interjected Ostagus. "Since we become time, and time becomes us, the task gets done when it's supposed to. We don't control it, but since it's us and we're it, time – or energy – is neither wasted nor gained, only used."

"Is time some kind of power?" asked Laney.

"Not superior to us, if that's what you mean. But it can be powerful, as it is on Earth. The difference is that on Earth, humans haven't yet made it a part of themselves as we have, so it seems like it has power over them. To us, it's something that we live with, something that's a part of us."

"Then turn this conversation back a few minutes."

"We can't, it's done," replied Ostagus. "We can't undo what has happened or passed."

"Why not?" asked Laney.

"It's a waste of energy, better yet, time. We don't waste anything that's part of us. We use it, or allow it just to be. Whether we are aware of it or not, it is with us."

"That's how everything remains a part of us, and we remain a part of everything," he continued, "by being."

The three of them walked past a painting of an elderly woman holding a branch in one hand and a clear vase of water in the other. She was wearing a gold dress that sparkled and glowed. She had an aura around her that reminded Laney of the one her mother, Diana-Mer, had. She wanted to tell both of them about it, but was becoming angry all over again. She thought they may know how she could see her mother again, but she didn't want that. Well, she did want it, but not now. Not until she could be sure of what she wanted to say. Actually, she wasn't sure if she would ever know what to say.

"Look familiar?" asked Kertar.

"Sort of, but not really. Should she?"

"Yes, she's your grandmother," he answered. "One of the founding mothers of Thrae."

"So I'm a descendant of hers," Laney mused. "A part of her."

"We believe she's part of us all. Especially you. You're of her blood."

Laney looked at the picture again. Her grandmother had blond hair and large hazel eyes. She seemed to be taller than Laney, and her mother for that matter, and had a hint of a smile on her face. Her jaw was strong and square, her head was cocked back slightly. She looked proud, determined, and although Laney kept trying to ignore it, a little mischievous.

"So she was one of the founders of Thrae?" asked Laney.

"Yes," replied Ostagus. "Many Earth-years ago this planet was barren and dark. From Earth it looked like nothing more than a 'dead' star. When your grandmother and her friends found it, they had another perception of it, and another idea for it. Come with us, we'll show you what it looked like, and what your grandmother made it."

They walked down the corridor to a large double door that led to a room that wasn't made of glass, but some kind of metal. Ostagus opened the door and a ray of light appeared at eye level. Ostagus held up his right hand to the light; the light turned off. The three of them walked in.

"Each person's hand is unique," said Ostagus. "The light 'read' my palm and granted me entry."

Laney turned around. The light had appeared again. She raised her hand to it. Her hand began to glow and the light became stronger. She tried to put her hand down to her side but couldn't. It felt like it was stuck in a jar. It didn't really hurt, and she sensed that she was not in any danger. She was more embarrassed than she was frightened.

"Laney," said Kertar, "you don't need to test the light. It senses that you're friendly, so it's merely holding you until one of us releases you. You need to realize that everything here isn't totally non-threatening to you. Although it senses that you're one of us, it hasn't had your hand in its bank for many years."

Kertar put his hand to the light and it went off. Laney rubbed her hand and her wrist. She blushed.

"Think of it as having your wrist slapped, gently of course," Ostagus said with a smile on his face. "That can happen here, too."

Ostagus walked over to a large circular bench in the middle of the room. He sat down, as did Kertar. Laney just stood there, a little frightened to go forward. Ostagus laughed and motioned her over. She sat between the two of them and didn't say a word. Now she wasn't quite as comfortable as she had been. She wasn't sure where her next "wrist-slapping" might occur and didn't want to take any chances.

Kertar put his arm around her and said: "A little caution goes a long way with you, doesn't it? That's good, Laney. Not just here, but anywhere you may be. Just don't carry your caution so far that you cease to trust us. If there had been a reason for you to avoid the light we would have told you."

"Then why didn't you tell me not to put my hand to the light?"

"Because you moved quickly into a relatively safe situation and because one light beam is worth a thousand words."

Laney crossed her arms and put her head down. She wasn't pouting, at least not in her mind, she was just trying to get control of herself. It was either that or tell Kertar and Ostagus what she thought of their little "lesson."

Calmly Ostagus said: "Laney, a lot of demands are going to be put on you soon. You have to minimize your mistakes. What's happened so far is nothing compared to what may happen. You'll need all the strength, which includes patience, that you can muster. Or that we can give you."

Laney looked at him and nodded. She didn't want to say it but she had heard it all before, and had a terrible feeling that she would be hearing it again. She looked at the panel of lights, switches and buttons in front of her and wished she knew which button to press to make her life go even a little bit back to the kind of life she knew on Earth. But as Ostagus said earlier, why waste the energy to turn back time? She knew she could only look at the past, live in the present and deal with whatever the future may be.

How it Began

Ostagus threw a switch and the ceiling became bright. He pressed a couple of buttons and the image of Laney's grandmother appeared in front of them.

"I am Maria. Many Earth-years ago my friends and I found this planet. It was dying. No, it was dead for all habitable purposes. The air contained particles that made it unbreathable, the water particles that were poisonous. We went back to our star and brought other friends. By opening the atmosphere we cleaned the air; through proper use of the air we cleaned the water. The soil remained unusable. We couldn't find a way to clean it. Another generation came after us. The land got cleaner, but we couldn't use it for planting. We couldn't even irrigate it because it would only re-poison the water.

"Then your mother, Diana-Mer, proposed that we live exclusively in the water. We were Thraeans, and we were able to adjust our bodies to the water. We weren't always mer-people. We were very much like humans, although biologically and intellectually superior. Initially we changed into mer-people by choice, but then our instincts took over and we didn't have to think about it. We naturally stayed as mer-people until we chose not to. The land has become somewhat cleaner now, but we have become so pure that we cannot live on it. That's were your story begins.

"You were sent to Earth at the age of five Earth-years because the cleaner the land got, the more aggressive the Garnots became, and the more obvious it became that we needed a power even greater than what we had collectively.

"You could only develop that power away from Thrae in a supportive environment. We chose your Earth family, although they don't know that. We erased your memory of Thrae so you could only be reached telepathically or while in a hypnotic trance.

"You were blood of our blood, a direct descendant of the line that began our exodus to the watery world which is ours. You had shown a tremendous power — a power we'd hoped would be our salvation when there was no other hope."

Her grandmother paused as she put her head down in deep thought. Laney wished she could interrupt and ask questions. Her grandmother continued.

"Knowing you, you're beyond thinking about yourself and you're wondering about the Garnots – who they are, where they're from."

Laney was shocked by Maria's comment, not realizing that insight was nothing new to her. Maria kept talking.

"The Garnots are a tribe of fallen Thraeans who refused to live in the water. They said it was too passive, so they decided to live on the poisoned land, and they became poisoned, too. Their goal became to rid the planet of the rest of us in any way they could. They began by trying to re-poison the air, but our system of purifying was too great. They tried to re-poison the water, but we were able to neutralize any poison they developed. Finally, they managed to develop a weapon that we cannot completely overcome. It's a weapon that, for lack of a better way of explanation, freezes us.

"We are pooling our skills – telekinesis, telepathy and many others – but the Garnots are able to wear away at them with their weapon. Any individual who is frozen has only half of his or her power when he or she is unfrozen. The Garnots are freezing more and more of us with each attack, so our collective strength is getting weaker and weaker.

"Now we are only good enough to keep them at bay. Even with Kertar's people, that has been the best we can do. It's gotten to the point where keeping them at bay is no longer enough. As the number of us who are untouched is reduced, our ability to keep them at bay decreases. We are at the point where we must stop them before they undo everything we've lived for, everything we hold dear, including life itself. We allowed you to become aware because you had to be brought back. The time had come.

"We had hoped that you could spend more time on Earth, learning in that environment, but we couldn't wait. The situation demands everything we have. It demands you.

"We must get the Garnots' weapon and destroy its configurations. We must also wipe out their memories of it. Even though they are fallen, they are still Threaeans. They cannot go back in time.

"Welcome home, Laney. We wanted you to come when there was more time to explain, but the Garnots have gotten stronger and faster than we had expected. Welcome home, my dear. Please help us."

Maria disappeared, as did the light on the ceiling. The three of them sat quietly. Kertar and Ostagus held their heads in their hands, gazing at the floor. They were breathing in unison and Laney thought they were in a trance.

She leaned back and said, "This is more incredible than anyone on Earth ever imagined. All the talk about my power, my being studied, prepared. They could never have expected this. Never."

"They didn't, at least not this soon," replied Kertar. "I told them some things about you, but only related to helping me get back here. They thought I could solve the problem on Thrae alone. Actually, so did I. I didn't have the chance to explain our bringing you back this quickly."

"You can tell them all about it when you go back, Laney," said Ostagus. "With everything Kertar told them, this one ought to have them engrossed more than ever."

"So you think I'll be going back?"

"Yes. I'm confident that you'll be able to handle things here. Afterwards you'll have to return to Earth for the same reason we sent you the first time. There may be other occasions when we'll need you, so you must keep yourself strong and ready."

Laney was proud to hear Ostagus talk to her that way. She believed him when he said she could do it. Now all she had to do was figure out a way to destroy the weapon, the configurations and the Garnots' memory. The more complicated this became, the more dependent she became. But she had Kertar, Ostagus and the people of Thrae. She wasn't sure how she could succeed, but she was sure she wouldn't fail.

Part III

Judith Galardi

The Plan

"When do we start?" she asked. "Better yet, where do we start?"

"We'll start immediately," replied Ostagus. "Our council has blueprints, maps and collective brainwave prints of the Garnots. You can go over those with them and they'll explain how you can accomplish your task."

"What do the Garnots look like?" she asked.

"Like us, with one exception. Their eyes are red. But that's another problem. They have the power to will their eyes to be the color of ours, unless you, that is, we, telepathically command them not to."

"Which is how they managed to infiltrate our life-spaces and learn what was deadly for us," Kertar said.

"You mean they could even be among us now?"

"Especially now," he answered. "That's why you must work quickly. Once they know you're here, they could turn the weapon on you, solely on you. Even with your level of power, they might be able to freeze you if they figure out the right intensity."

"Let's go to the council," said Ostagus. "There's really no time to lose."

They walked down the corridor and passed by the room where the Thraeans had their collective healing session. The room was empty except for a couple of people who were talking quietly. Laney wondered if they were actually Thraeans or if they were Garnots. She wanted to send them commands telepathically to let their eyes be their normal color but she didn't. She realized she couldn't suspect everyone she saw, but at the same time she knew she had to look for signs that some of people around her might not be who they pretended to be. She wondered what those signs might be: questions that were too pointed about her power, too much interest in her life on Earth, extraordinary interest in her "task?"

She turned to Ostagus and said, "Isn't there anything else but the red eyes to identify a Garnot?"

"Yes," he said. "They cannot keep eye contact for more than an Earth-minute. Not only can telepathy change their eye color, but a Thraean looking into them for that amount of time can make them change."

They walked into a round room surrounded by the light beam she had been through earlier. The three of them put their hands to the light and they were able to pass through. There were a few people in the room sitting around an oval table. On the table were diagrams, maps and long strips of paper with thin black lines on them. The strips of paper looked like the ones from her brainwave tests on Earth. The ceiling was the same dome shape as in the room they had left. There were several pictures on the ceiling of Thraeans, although they could have been Garnots. Laney couldn't tell because their eyes were the normal color.

The people turned when the three-some arrived. Some nodded, one smiled, another just sat quietly and looked at Laney. Laney was a little disappointed that her mother wasn't there. She kept wondering when she would see her again. She wasn't feeling quite as angry. She felt as if she understood her mother a little more. But Laney still wanted some answers from her; that hadn't changed.

Ostagus pointed to a chair at the head of the table and said, "You may sit there, Laney. We need to begin."

Laney brushed by a couple of the people as she headed for the chair. She noticed that their skin felt a little cooler than Earth-skin. She thought it was because they were mer-people and were used to being in the water. The truth was that those people had already been frozen once, and they needed to give her their information immediately because they hardly had the strength to remember it. She sat at the head of the table and looked around at them. No one spoke. She began to feel uncomfortable.

Finally, she sucked in her bottom lip, wrinkled her forehead, looked around at them all and in a deep voice said, "Hi, I'm Laney. I'm here to save Thrae."

They all broke into laughter except for one person who remained quiet and rather stiff.

Laney laughed and sat down. *At least they haven't completely lost their senses of humor*, she thought. She knew none of this would be easy, but she needed to let them know she was willing to try.

"Seriously, I am here to save Thrae," she continued. "We are all here to save Thrae, so we'll work together. I promise to do everything in my power, ahhh, powers, to do what you ask, but each of you must help me in any way you can. I can't do this alone."

Some of the people sat back in their chairs, a little stunned by Laney's straightforwardness. The one who had remained stiff began to tap his fingers on the table.

He cried out, "How can we expect this mere child, virtually an Earth-child, to save Thrae! What idiocy! We'd be better off doing it ourselves!"

"We've tried it ourselves and failed," replied the woman at Laney's right. "In fact it was our postponement of bringing her here that has made matters as bad as they are now! We can't do it alone, Lonan, we've tried and failed."

Lonan looked directly at Laney and said, "Okay little girl, just what do you want us to do?"

He was almost snarling. Laney knew he was being cynical, but why not? How could a young girl do so much? On the other hand, how could he be so sure she'd fail? She was going to lash out at him but caught Ostagus from the corner of her eye. His jaw was firm and he looked as if he was going to shout at Lonan any second.

She knew her anger would do nothing but make the situation much worse.

Suddenly she remembered the two birds flying together and she said: "Help me so I can help you. At this point you haven't anything to lose since what you've been doing has failed. Give me a chance before you judge me. If I fail you can go back to your methods. Give me a chance because I may be your last chance."

Lonan's eyes flashed bright yellow. Laney was a little frightened.

"It's okay, Laney. When someone from Thrae has dealt with their anger their eyes flash yellow," said Kertar.

"It's good you've come to your senses," he said to Lonan. "You've come this far, you may as well make the whole journey."

Lonan put his head in his hands and rested his elbows on the table. He said softly, "I'm one of the original members of the water-life, Laney. I joined shortly after your grandmother and the others provided for it. I've seen this planet emerge from its infancy. Everything I've ever lived for is here. Everything I am is here. I can't bear to lose my friends, my planet. Ours is a culture too precious to lose."

Then he cried. His tears looked like crystals falling from his eyes. Other people in the room went over to comfort him by putting their arms around him and rubbing his back.

He stopped crying and said, "I was present at your birth, Laney. You are from the blood line of the most gifted. You may have a chance. I'll support you in any way I can."

"We all will," said the woman who had come to Laney's defense. "I am Eve, a friend of your mother. I'll be presenting you with the maps of where we think the freezing devices may be located. By the way, I hope to get to know you better after you're task is accomplished."

"Thanks for the vote of confidence, Eve," answered Laney. "I'm sure we will get to know each other better."

"Then we'd better get to work now," she responded.

Eve spread out large sheets of paper outlined with mountains, hills and various bodies of water. The mountains and hills were somewhat elevated on the paper. There was an "X" in the middle of one body of water, which Laney assumed was the life-space she was in. There were arrows and circles near a range of mountains that Laney figured had to be the location of the device, but there were more locations than one.

"You probably understand basically what this means," Eve said to Laney. "We are where the 'X' is. The arrows show the best way for you to approach the cave. The circles indicate the three caves where the devices may be. We say 'devices' because two early versions of the device are there to trick us. They are not as powerful but they emit the same configuration of rays as the real one so we can't tell them apart. For whatever help it may be, take this map with you. You probably won't need it because you'll be able to tell which way to go by the lights and the gases."

Then a man with a moustache and beard spoke. "I am Quar, head of the defense system here. Each of the caves is guarded by specially trained Garnots who have orders to capture you alive, only alive. I suppose there's some comfort there. There's only one way you can protect yourself, by rendering them unconscious through eye contact. Unfortunately, there is a rumor that they have devised special lenses that can reverse your gaze back to you; thus, you would render yourself unconscious. We have no way of knowing whether or not these lenses work. Actually, we doubt they will work since they've never encountered you, but we aren't completely sure. There's only one way you can find out, the most dangerous way."

"Is there going to be anyone with me?" Laney asked.

"Of course," said Quar, "but only up to the point of entry to the three caves. After that, you'll be on your own, until you disintegrate each device."

"You see," continued Eve, "the devices produce an unidentified gas. The Garnots are immune to it, but to a Thraean it can be crippling. You have immunity to it. We don't know why or how, we just know that you do."

"How do you know?" asked Laney.

"You came through it when you made the transition back. It's part of the freezing device. The device throws it off when it's in use. When you arrived the gas was in the water. It didn't bother you."

Laney remembered how the water churned and what the life-space looked like when she was brought in. She wondered for a moment how Ostagus could have been in the water, but figured that he must have stayed at a depth where it was safe. She felt guilty that she suspected Ostagus of being a spy. She felt a hand on her shoulder. She jumped.

"Laney, don't let this throw you. You have our support."

She turned her head. It was Ostagus. He pressed her shoulder just hard enough for her to notice. He looked into her eyes for a few seconds then down at the drawing.

"We've been working on this plan for quite a while. We have just about everything worked out."

"Just about?" asked Laney. "What's missing?"

"How to get to you if you're captured," said Quar. "With those gases around you, and your being away from the water, we won't be able to penetrate the caves. You'll be stuck there until—."

"Until what?" Laney questioned.

"Until you figure out a way to get loose, or they decide to release you," said Quar.

"How likely would my release be?"

"Not very," he responded.

"There is hope, though," said Eve. "When you reach the device, or shall I say, devices, you must disintegrate them completely. Nothing can be left.

When you disintegrate, make sure the energy you get from them goes directly to you. Don't redirect it anywhere but to yourself. That way you'll have enough power that even the Garnots, special lenses or not, won't be able to stop you. From there, the rest will seem easy. As you eliminate the devices, you'll eliminate the gases. When that happens, we'll be there. We'll collectively work to eradicate the Garnots' memory while Quar and his friends seek out the blueprints and configurations."

"How will you join me?" asked Laney. "Won't the Garnots have the strength until I disintegrate the devices? You can't go in the caves until everything is clear."

"That's true," Eve answered. "But there's an underground river to the caves. We can stay in the water at a safe depth until the gases have been cleared. Once that's done, we'll be able to go for the documents."

Laney sat back in her chair and looked into the eyes of the people around the table. Eve looked tired; Quar looked concerned. Kertar just sat with his head in his hands and winked at Laney. His eyes were bright and he was trying to smile, but he couldn't. Lonan had his eyes closed and his hands were folded in a prayer-like position. Ostagus looked fully alert as he folded his arms and stared at the plan in front of Laney.

Laney wondered about him again. She hadn't given much thought to how much eye contact she'd had with him. Yet he was very helpful when he got her to the life-space. With everything else she had to do, she decided to try to notice him a little more.

Lonan interrupted her train of thought. "There is one other thing," he said. "After you've absorbed the devices, you'll have all the information about it; thus, you'll be able to reconstruct it and put it to use in any way you choose. No one can stop you. The choice will be yours."

"Won't you have the collective knowledge from the blueprints and configurations?"

"No," he replied. "The information will be scattered, and meaningless. To true Thraeans, weapons of destruction don't make sense, so we won't even keep the information once we get it. We'll convert the energy from it to cleaning the land and helping the sick ones get well."

"What makes you think I might use the information to make something destructive?"

"Because you came through the gases unharmed," Lonan replied. "There's no way for us to know if your power got you through or if somehow you've been poisoned too, thus becoming one of them."

"I'm a true Thraean. I'll convert the energy to myself and help you rebuild Thrae."

"I hope so," he replied.

Laney didn't like being doubted. Now she felt as if she was being spied on. She was more willing than ever to prove herself, to save Thrae. She had to. Then she could finally be a part of her people.

Everyone in the room was looking down at the diagrams and maps on the table. Only Eve was looking at Laney. Eve was a lovely woman – about five feet, eight inches tall, long dark brown hair, large green-gray eyes. She had a soft, warm voice. She looked deeply into Laney's eyes as if she could see what was written in Laney's heart.

Eve spoke: "Laney, it's not that anyone here, and that includes Lonan, doubts you. You've been through a lot, and some of it we cannot explain, which makes it difficult for us to know how you'll react in certain situations. On the other hand, you're dependent on us, too. If we can't reach you inside the cave, we don't know what will happen to you. We don't want you to fail. Not just for the sake of Thrae, but because even though some of us don't know you at all, we don't want to lose you. Anyone who shows the courage and trust you've shown already is deserving of our friendship and affection."

Laney looked at her and nodded, then she put her arms around her. "I know how you feel. I don't want to fail either. We all have a lot to do, a lot to share. When do I go to the caves?"

"Tonight," answered Quar. "When the moons are full."

"How many moons are there?" Laney asked.

"Seven," he replied. "We like to think there's one for each of our founding mothers."

Mother, Laney thought to herself. When would she see Diana-Mer again? Laney wanted to see her before she left, but she was afraid to ask about Diana-Mer. Laney was holding herself back. She still didn't know how to handle her mother. It didn't occur to her that Diana-Mer may have had her own reasons for being distant with her. Nor did she know that Diana-Mer had been with her the whole time – as Eve.

The Infiltration

Kertar, Ostagus, Eve, Quar and about twenty Thraeans joined Laney that evening for the swim to the caves. The Thraeans were very excited. They all had wide belts wrapped around their waists with various instruments on them. One of the instruments was a box with a gauge on it, like a light meter, or a Geiger counter.

A Thraean spoke: "These are not instruments of destruction, but instruments of rebuilding. Once you've eliminated the devices and the gases, and we've located and destroyed the blueprints, we'll begin the collective thought process of wiping out the memory of the devices from the Garnots. This gauge you see is a meter that will measure the memory waves of the Garnots. When it hits the number ten, we know their collective memory of the device is gone. Once that's finished, we can work with them on a peaceful settlement of this problem."

"You mean you won't try to control them with your minds?" Laney asked.

"No," said Kertar. "That would be substituting one oppression for another. We don't intend to conquer them in that way. We only wish to teach them about our ways and to show them there's space here for all of us. It will be up to them to decide how to manage that knowledge."

"But they'll also be aware that although we are a peaceful people we won't just give up," said Eve. "They'll understand that we will use our powers if necessary to maintain our lives and culture."

Laney nodded in approval. She realized that even a peaceful race like the Thraeans had to defend themselves and that it took a great sensitivity to know when to put the power to use. It reminded her of the classes she had when she was on Earth, how the teachers would stress that with freedom comes immense responsibility. She felt proud to be a member of both races. Not one who had to choose between the two, but one who had the qualities of both.

Quar looked into the sky through a telescope. There were seven moons, each glowing yellow-orange. They were all about the same size and seemed equidistant from one another and Thrae. She wondered which one belonged to her grandmother. She hoped it was the one in the middle, the one that seemed to give the others a sense of position.

"It's time to swim to the caves, my friends," he said to everyone. "Let's all keep together. If somehow the device is turned on us, we must dive directly into the reef. Keep an eye on each other. If one of us freezes we must turn our thoughts to Laney. She must get to the caves. We'll come back for the wounded later."

"I'm ready when you are," she said. "I'm eager to serve you."

"Was that 'serve' us or 'save' us?" asked Ostagus.

They all smiled, shook hands or embraced, and walked to the edge of the sea. It was peach colored, as it was when Laney first entered it from Earth. She'd make it, she told herself. She was sure.

Everyone in the group turned into a mer-person as soon as they hit the water and swam toward the open sea. The map showed the caves to be only a couple of miles from the life-space. Laney couldn't understand why the Garnots had become greedy and oppressive, but she knew that sometimes happens to people. Power? Maybe. Or maybe just to make themselves feel superior to a race that was superior in such a humble way that the Garnots felt ashamed because they were no longer a part of them. Regardless, she hoped she could be part of the peace process once the devices and documents were destroyed. Helping the Garnots relearn the ways of the Thraeans would also be a way for Laney to learn, not only more about the Thraeans, but about peace.

The group swam above what looked like a large statue of a mer-woman. Laney pointed down at it. Ostagus, who had been swimming behind her, said, "The mer-woman is a popular figure around here. That one sank during transport from another life-space. We decided to leave it where it is. After all, isn't that where a mer-person belongs?"

Laney tried to say, "That's true," but got a mouth full of water instead. She coughed up the water and quickly closed her mouth.

Ostagus laughed and said, "Talking under water is a skill that takes a little while to master. We'll work on it later. Talk to me telepathically instead."

She thought, *never mind, I'll concentrate on swimming instead*, and continued forward. Then she telepathically said to Ostagus, "There's a difference between my sending you telepathic messages and just thinking, isn't there?"

"Usually," he answered. "But every now and again a 'private' thought gets through. Some of our scientists believe it's because deep down inside we want the other person to know our thoughts anyway."

Laney wondered if that was why Ostagus approached her at the meeting after she thought he might be a spy. There was no way for her to know for sure, not now anyway. There was enough for her to do.

There was a vague image of a mountain range about five hundred yards ahead. It looked like something out of a dream. It almost seemed to move, although Laney knew it was an optical trick caused by the water. The closer they got the slower they swam. She could see huge holes in the sides of the mountains, just as the map had shown. They swam toward the hole on the far left, the one that led to the caves. Laney's heart began to beat faster. She wasn't sure if it was fear or excitement. It was both.

They swam inside the hole and climbed out onto the rocks. "This is as far as we can go," said Eve. "We'll be waiting in the water below.

As soon as we see the third set of lights flash, we'll know you've disintegrated all the devices. Lonan and his people will get to the documents. Kertar, Ostagus and I will come after you. Good luck, my darling, our thoughts and wishes are with you."

Some of the others patted Laney on the back, others smiled and nodded. Kertar put his arms around her and said, "I only wish I could join you now as I did when you were on Earth. Be safe."

Ostagus looked directly into her eyes for a couple of minutes and said, "I'll be expecting three sets of flashing lights very soon. You'd better go." He looked into her eyes for a couple more minutes then he winked at her. She was relieved; she knew he wasn't a spy.

Lonan had remained in the water the whole time. He said, "We've got to go. We'll be caught if we stay here. You never know when they'll set off the device."

At that moment the earth started to shake and a cloud of gas came rolling through the cave. "Dive! Into the water!" one of the Thraeans yelled. Within a couple of seconds they had all disappeared safely into the water, except for Laney. She covered her eyes and peeked through her fingers to see how thick the cloud was. She noticed that it didn't bother her at all, not even her eyes. She walked down the path toward a "Y." There she would go to the right, toward the cave that was supposed to contain one of the devices.

She got to the point where she would make her turn, but noticed that the cloud was coming from the left. She wasn't sure which path to take. She tried to reach Quar telepathically; she couldn't. Suddenly Eve seemed to say to her, "It's a trick. They rerouted the cloud. Go to the right."

Laney went to the right. The cave curved and jutted this way and that, and there were boulders and holes and pits in the way as well. She noticed a dim yellow light pulsating around the next bend. She was getting closer to the turn when she saw the shadow of a man. *One of the guards*, she thought to herself. She stopped for a moment. *I don't know if he's wearing the special lenses that reverse my gaze or not. I'll have to chance it.*

She glanced around the corner and saw him. He was about six feet, seven inches tall and carried what looked like a rifle, except the tip was glowing blue. He had red eyes. Behind him was an enormous machine that looked like a telescope with a control panel. It pulsated a yellow light and had eight smaller tubes coming out of each side. Puffs of gas were coming out of the tubes.

Laney watched the guard pace back and forth. He wasn't aware of her. She had to disarm him but knew if she disintegrated his weapon, he'd find her. If he was wearing those special lenses he could capture her. If she didn't disarm him he'd become aware of her once she started to disintegrate the device. She decided to go for his weapon first. At least he wouldn't be able to use that.

Laney peered around the corner again. The guard's back was to her. She concentrated on the weapon and it began to glow. He turned around suddenly, reached for it, but it had already disappeared. She hid behind a boulder. He came around one side of it and she went around the other. She concentrated on the device. He was getting closer. The device turned a bright green then disappeared. The Garnot grabbed Laney.

"So it's you! We weren't sure you actually existed, but here you are.

You won't be getting any farther than this!"

She stared into his eyes. Everything went black.

Being Captive

Laney woke up in a small dark room. There were no windows, only a door. She tried to stand up but her legs wobbled and she fell back into a seated position. As she leaned her head against the wall, she thought about the events that led to her being a captive. She remembered looking into the Garnot's eyes; obviously, they did have the lenses she had heard about. Her eyes hurt, as if there was soap in them. She drew her knees to her chest and rested her chin on them. She thought: *Problem one – how to get away. Problem two – how to get by those lenses. Problem three – how to get to the next device.*

There was a rattle at the door and soon a Garnot entered. Laney didn't want to look into his eyes, so she continued to stare at the floor.

"Well, Laney," he said. "Did you enjoy your nap?" He snorted as he laughed at her. "After all," he continued mockingly, "a little girl like you probably still needs her naps."

She looked up at him, but wasn't thinking in terms of rendering him unconscious. As she continued to look directly into his eyes, she could see the lenses. They were clear, like contact lenses, and she noticed that one of the edges didn't completely cover the cornea. That gave her an idea.

"You're right," she replied. "Why don't you sing me a lullaby?"

"Oh, a sarcastic one, eh? I'm not surprised. The Thraeans think you're so great. That must have gone to your head."

"You Garnots are really on to something with those lenses. Are you all wearing them or are you the lucky one?"

"A couple of us have them, but what difference does it make to you? Even one of us wearing them can stop you."

"You never know what can happen, right? After all I made it far enough to destroy a device."

"But that will be all you destroy. And you only destroyed one of the fakes. We're still in control, and with you as our hostage, we'll be in total control."

Laney noticed he was holding one of those rifle-like weapons. She said, "If you're in so much control, why do you need that gun? You're wearing the lenses. I'm helpless against you."

"This isn't a gun. It's an opti-stun. The light from it can stun anyone, a Thraean, a Garnot, maybe even you."

Laney looked into his eyes again. The lens still left a small part of his eye uncovered. She concentrated on the opti-stun and directed its ray toward his eyes. She willed him to be silent. At first the ray was reflected, but not away from that small corner. She directed it totally to that spot. He jumped toward her but she moved away. Suddenly he was frozen in a lurching position. She took the opti-stun from him and slung it over her shoulder. She looked around the corner. There was another guard about ten feet down the corridor sitting in front of another door. There was a faint yellow light and a smoky gas coming from underneath the door, so she knew that was the way to the next device. At first she thought she'd just fire the opti-stun from where she was, but she figured he might be able to call out to others. She decided to try to get him to her cell, then stun him.

She concentrated on the guard in her room. Although he was unconscious, she willed him to speak: "Irum, Irum. Come to Laney's cell. I need your help."

Laney could hear the guard coming toward her. She sat in the corner, near the guard, to look as if he was bending over her.

Irum entered and said: "What's wrong with you? Can't you even handle a thirteen-year-old girl?"

Laney jumped out with the opti-stun aimed at his eyes. He was wearing the lenses, but the brightness of the ray seemed to be penetrating them anyway.

She willed him to be silent and said: "You invented lenses that I couldn't penetrate but that your own weapons could! I'm surprised you're all so trusting."

Irum was bent over at the waist with his eyes agape and his mouth open, teeth clenched. Laney looked out the door and saw that no one else was around. She noticed a box in Irum's pocket. It was some kind of gauge. She decided to take it and experiment with it later, even though she didn't know what it was. She'd find out as soon as she reached the door down the hall.

At the door, she looked through a small window. There was a guard with a panel of buttons, switches and lights in front of him. Behind the panel was another device. Laney squinted as she looked at the panel. It had the letters DVT on the top of it, just as they appeared on the top of the gauge. *I've got nothing to lose,* she thought to herself, then turned the dial on the gauge. A bright green light jetted from the panel into the eyes of the guard. He put his arms in front of his eyes.

"Turn it off," he screamed. "Turn it off!"

"Open the door and I'll turn it off!" answered Laney.

"I can't. Not with the light the way it is. At least turn it down. Please!"

Laney turned the dial a bit to the left and the guard opened the door, still shielding his eyes. "Please, turn it all the way off!"

Laney grabbed the opti-stun from his belt and said, "Not until you answer some questions."

"Okay, okay. But be quick."

"Is this the true device?"

"Yes."

"Then where's the last dummy?"

"We dismantled it. The parts are down that corridor. We were going to incorporate it into this one to make it twice as powerful."

"What about this panel?"

"It controls the device, as does the gauge you're holding. The gauge also activates the techni-guard, that bright light that's in my eyes. It prevents anyone from destroying the device."

"So if I destroy the panel or the device, everything will be destroyed, right?"

"Right."

Laney looked into his eyes and knew she had to believe him. She put him in a trance and concentrated on the panel. It turned a translucent purple then a transparent green, then became encased in bright yellow light. In a jolt of clear white light the panel and the device disappeared. She looked at the gauge. It completely disappeared from her hand.

She looked into the guard's eyes and released him from his trance.

"Come with me to those dismantled parts," she said to him. "I still have work to do."

They walked down the passage together. She aimed the opti-stun at him but concentrated on the device that was piled against the wall. In a flash of white light it disappeared.

She was quite surprised at how quickly it happened.

Suddenly, Eve and Ostagus appeared. "Don't be surprised by the speed at which you disintegrated this last device," said Eve. "Remember, now you have the energy that was once locked in the devices."

"How did you get here so soon?" asked Laney.

"Our knowledge of the devices was a little off. Once you disintegrated the real device, the rays from the dummy were weak enough for us to work safely. Our friends have already located the documents and are destroying them. Everyone in our life-space is starting to erase the device from the Garnots' memories. It won't take long."

Laney looked at the guard and his expression was no longer fearful but peaceful.

"Thank you," he said. "Thank all of you. Some of us wanted our independence, yes, but we didn't want it to cost you yours, or your lives, in the process. Lonan was the one who wanted it that way."

"Lonan!" shouted Laney. "Lonan wanted it?"

"Yes, Laney," said Ostagus. "He was not only the infiltrator, but he's the one who started all of this."

"Why?"

"He didn't think our culture ought to survive. 'It was too weak,' he said, 'too innocent, too forgiving.'"

"Then you'll forgive him, after all he's done?"

"Of course we will," answered Eve. "He'll have his choice – either live among us in peace or leave for another planet. It's up to him."

"You're not going to punish him?"

"Having been found out and losing are punishment enough, don't you think?"

"I suppose. But what if he tries to take over again?"

"Then we'll accept his challenge again, and he'll lose again. But we don't think he will try. Already he realizes how wrong he was. He's back at our life-space, contemplating the choice."

"Do you think he'll stay?"

"We don't know," replied Ostagus. "He knows he's welcome, but he also knows the rules. It depends on how he wants to live and what he wants to put his energy into."

"And now I must ask your forgiveness, Laney," said Eve.

Laney looked to her but she had changed. Her hair was brown and curly. She had a golden aura around her. She was Diana-Mer! She walked toward Laney with her arms open for an embrace. Laney stepped back.

"Mother! It's been you all along?"

"Yes. I was afraid you wouldn't let me help you had you known who I really was. Please forgive me, not only for deceiving you, but for leaving you so abruptly."

"Why? Why didn't you tell me?"

"There was no time, and I knew we'd be together again someday."

"But why?"

"To make you strong enough to handle this situation – and others that may be in our future."

"But just to leave me on Earth, no explanation, nothing."

"Sometimes separation is like that. There is no time and we must go on, as cruel as it sounds, as painful as it may be. In this case we were lucky. I knew we'd be together again."

Laney stood quietly. There were tears in her eyes and in Diana-Mer's.

Diana-Mer shook her head and said: "I love you, Laney. I always have. Leaving you wasn't easy. Being with you now is something I have waited for since the moment I sent you away. But you're here and so am I. I need your forgiveness, and I hope, over time, you'll love me too."

Laney turned to Ostagus, who was smiling but also had tears in his eyes. She put her arms around him and cried. Diana-Mer was crying too. Ostagus cleared his throat, wiped the tears from his eyes and held her tightly.

"It's okay, Laney," he said. "I know how you feel. I've been aware of this since before you were sent to Earth. I'm your father."

Laney cried for a few more minutes, wiped her eyes and stepped back. Diana-Mer approached her again. Laney put her arms around her and sighed. She felt relieved. Finally she knew her Thrae parents. Even though it was hard for her to think of them as parents, it was a comforting thought that she was part of these two people.

She wanted to tell them so but Ostagus said: "Don't say anything, Laney. Let's just go back to our life-space. We feel very much a part of you, too."

The three of them walked through the cave back to where they started. The bright, pulsating lights were gone, the air was clean and any Garnot they ran into would humbly nod his or her head and make room for them to pass.

They arrived at their place of entry. Quar and Kertar were there. They each smiled at the threesome and dove into the water. Laney and her Thrae parents followed. Quar and Kertar were swimming quickly, but Laney, Ostagus and Diana-Mer swam slowly, since they just wanted to be alone and quiet together. They passed over the statue of the mer-woman. It was graceful in the swirling sand. Diana-Mer dove down toward it and signaled to Laney to follow. She did, and when she got close Laney realized that it looked like her!

"We've all been waiting for you Laney," said Diana-Mer. "We knew you'd be back. You're more beautiful than our best sculptor could show."

Laney took Diana-Mer by the hand and they swam toward Ostagus. Together, as one, they swam home.

A Different Good-bye

They emerged onto the platform at the life-space. All of the Threaeans looked happy, and they stopped whatever they were doing and applauded as Laney walked down the corridor. One person was holding a sign that read, "Hey, Laney. What took you so long?" Laney laughed when she saw it and said, "I stopped to smell the flowers."

They got to a room made of red crystal. Laney sat on a bench as her parents were putting some things in a sleeve.

"What happened to my grandmother? Is she dead?" asked Laney.

"Oh no," answered Ostagus, "she's off discovering another planet. And this time, **this time**," he said in a kind of false anger, "she didn't leave a mailing address." (Actually his anger wasn't entirely exaggerated, but that's another story.)

They all laughed as Laney thought about the woman with the twinkle in her eye and a glow in her heart.

"You may meet her yet," continued Ostagus. "She never fails to amaze anyone, least of all her own daughter and son-in-law."

"Why did she name this planet Thrae?" asked Laney.

"Because it's a mirror image of Earth," answered Diana-Mer. "A mirror image of its best qualities. It was her idea to send you to Earth. She knew you'd be able to manage there, to flourish, to be strong enough to come back."

"And that's why you've got to go back," said Ostagus. "You must let the people know what's happened here, what's happened to you, and how we'll be living in peace again."

"So you do want me to leave again?"

"Yes, my love," replied Ostagus. "If you return there, you'll be able to keep your powers and return to us."

Laney leaned back. She knew it would be this way. She knew the only way she could be a part of Thrae was to stay away from it until those times when there was little hope.

"On the other hand," said Diana-Mer, "now that you know about us here, we'll be able to contact you more, both telepathically and in spirit. You'll be open to our communications and thoughts."

She knew then that they were packing that sleeve for her. In a way she couldn't wait to get back to her family, friends and school. Her life was waiting for her on Earth. Her life on Thrae would always be there.

"What are you putting in the sleeve?" asked Laney.

"It's a machine you would call 'DVD player' on Earth, but ours is a little more advanced. Be sure Dr. Bucci gets to take it apart, and remind him that he hasn't put it back together correctly unless there are a few pieces lying around when he's done."

Laney laughed. Diana-Mer smiled, but then had a more serious tone as she said, "This recording will explain what's been happening here and how the peace process works. Some people on Earth seem to need a few lessons in it."

Diana-Mer handed her the sleeve and the three of them walked down a hallway. Ostagus said, "Remember, Laney, don't misuse your powers. They're stronger than you've ever known them to be, but that makes them more vulnerable to being taken for granted."

Laney knew what they meant. Sometimes being proud can destroy exactly what the individuals are proud of, unless they keep in mind their limits.

They got to an archway made of some kind of gel. The water splashed behind it.

"This is a time/water channel, Laney. Although you don't recognize it, it's what you came through to get here. Just dive in and in a brief moment, you'll be back at school."

"I don't know what to say," Laney commented. Then she looked at them both and they joined hands.

"We can understand that," said Diana-Mer. "We'll be in touch often. Remember, we're only a thought-projection away."

"That's true, Laney," said Ostagus. "In fact, we may show up so often you'll be telling us to go back."

"I doubt that," said Laney.

"I don't," said Diana-Mer. "All parents tend to get in the way every once in a while, don't they?"

Laney was a little surprised but then laughed, knowing that even the best-intentioned person can complicate things.

She nodded and said jokingly in a demanding voice, "You're right. I hope you two will behave yourselves.

And please, keep this planet in order, will you!"

"We will," said Ostagus, "and if things go wrong, we know where you live."

"Good-bye Laney," said Diana-Mer. "You'll be in my thoughts and dreams."

"Good-bye," said Ostagus. "Our love is always with you."

"Good-bye to you both. I'll send you my thoughts often."

The three embraced and Diana-Mer put the sleeve across Laney's back and tied it in front. "This shouldn't get in your way," she said softly. "You're quite the swimmer."

Laney hugged her again and dove into the water. In what seemed like just a couple of seconds, she could hear Dr. Bucci's voice.

Epilogue

"Are you all right? Laney, are you all right?" Dr. Bucci was shouting as Laney swam to the edge of the pool. She reached for Dr. Bucci's hand and allowed him to help her out.

"I'm fine," she answered. "Just fine."

"Where have you been? You seemed to disappear for a couple of seconds. The water became misty and I couldn't see you."

"I wasn't there," she answered.

"Did you go underwater?" he asked.

"No," answered Laney as she put on her robe. "I went to Thrae."

"Thrae!"

"Yes, Thrae."

"How? We were supposed to explain…" Dr. Bucci's voice tapered off as though he was immersed in his own thoughts.

"This'll explain everything," she answered, giving him the sleeve. "It'll teach us all something."

She walked toward the door and asked, "Would you like to escort me to my room? I think I'd better change."

Dr. Bucci smiled and nodded. "I don't intend to let you out of my sight."

"You may not have that choice all the time," replied Laney.

They walked down the hall to her room. Students were passing her on both sides and one bumped into her.

"Hey!" said Dr. Bucci. "Watch where you're going!"

"Take it easy, Dr. Bucci," said Laney. "That was nothing. In fact, it's like old times."

They were in the corridor a few doors from her room when Charles came charging toward them. He was smiling broadly and waving his arms. *Maybe he showed some secret power*, thought Laney.

"Laney, guess what?" he shouted.

"You moved a mountain with one arm tied behind your back," she responded with a smile.

"Better than that. Erin's going to go to the dance with me Saturday night."

"That's great," she said. "It's better than moving a mountain."

"Huh?" said Charles.

"Nothing, nothing, that's wonderful news."

Laney was thrilled for Charles, and she was quite happy to be back with the usual concerns in her life again. She couldn't wait to see the expression on Michael's face when she told him what happened. She noticed Dr. Henderson coming toward her.

"How about some more hypnosis, Laney?" he asked.

"Ahhh, later, Dr. Henderson," said Dr. Bucci. "I think we'd better leave that alone for a while. Let's get together and watch this recording instead."

They reached Laney's door. She opened it and noticed how the sun drenched her room in brightness. She looked in the mirror and she seemed different. She wasn't sure, but she was almost certain there was a golden aura around her.

"You look radiant," said Dr. Bucci. "Travel serves you well." Then he paused and said, "Will you stay with us?"

"Until I'm needed again on Thrae, or anywhere else I may be called to."

Suddenly her grandmother appeared in the mirror. She smiled at Laney and said: "That's the spirit, Laney. Be willing to accept challenges. One thing for certain, life will never be dull!"

Grandmother winked and disappeared. Laney looked at Dr. Bucci and said, "Think of it this way, you haven't lost a student, you've gained a space traveler!"

Dr. Bucci leaned back in his chair for a moment and said, "Well, at least we know that you're more challenging than we originally thought. That ought to keep us on our toes."

"Not to mention at the edge of your seat!" replied Laney.

At that, Laney asked permission to call her Earth parents. They'd have a lot to talk about and, Laney hoped, a whole lot to do.

About the Author

Judith Galardi is a published poet with numerous poems and a chapbook to her credit. She enjoys performance and doing volunteer work. Much of that work includes young people. Ms. Galardi, who recently received her Master's Degree in Library and Information Science, has a special interest in literature for children and teens.

She lives with her husband, daughter, and dog.

To her knowledge, no one she knows is from outer space.

Printed in the United States
1316600003B/79-189

9 781403 308160